AFTERLIFE

AFTERLIFE

a novel by

Julia Alvarez

ALGONQUIN BOOKS OF CHAPEL HILL   2020

Published by
Algonquin Books of Chapel Hill
Post Office Box 2225
Chapel Hill, North Carolina 27515-2225

a division of
Workman Publishing
225 Varick Street
New York, New York 10014

Excerpt from "Little Gidding" from *Four Quartets* by T. S. Eliot. Copyright © 1942 by T. S. Eliot,
renewed 1970 by Esme Valerie Eliot. Reprinted by permission of Houghton Mifflin Harcourt
Publishing Company. All rights reserved.

My thanks to Anita Barrows and Joanna Macy, for permission to quote from their translations of
Rainer Maria Rilke; Robert Hass, for permission to quote his translation of Issa's haiku; Coleman
Barks, for permission to quote his translation of Rumi; John Lanchester, for permission to quote
his words regarding climate change; Claudia Pierpont Roth, for permission to quote her remarks
on Black English. Gracias to Roberto and Susan Veguez, Sheriff Don Keeler, Susan Randall, Nancy
Stevens, Julia Doucet, Mike Kiernan, Misse Smith, Ceidy, Marlene, and las Gallinas. And to Amy
Gash, my editor, for her skilled eye, indispensable help, good humor, and guidance. Most of all to
Stuart Bernstein, agent and angel, for his support through thick and thin and very skinny, for his
faith and his affection for the books, loved into becoming better than they otherwise would be. And
as always, gracias to la Virgencita de la Altagracia, with me through all these pages, and beyond.

LIBRARY OF CONGRESS CATALOGING-IN-PUBLICATION DATA

Names: Alvarez, Julia, author.
Title: Afterlife : a novel / by Julia Alvarez.
Description: First edition. | Chapel Hill : Algonquin Books of Chapel Hill, 2020. |
Summary: "A literature professor tries to rediscover who she is after the sudden death
of her husband, even as a series of family and political jolts force her to ask what we
owe those in crisis in our families, biological or otherwise"—Provided by publisher.
Identifiers: LCCN 2019042436 | ISBN 9781643750255 (hardcover) |
ISBN 9781643750507 (ebook)
Subjects: LCSH: Domestic fiction.
Classification: LCC PS3551.L845 A69 2020 | DDC 813/.54—dc23
LC record available at https://lccn.loc.gov/2019042436

10 9 8 7 6 5 4 3 2 1
First Edition

Maury

We die with the dying:
See, they depart, and we go with them.
We are born with the dead:
See, they return, and bring us with them.

—T. S. ELIOT, *The Four Quartets*, "Little Gidding"

CONTENTS

AFTERLIFE

Broken English

She is to meet him / a place they often choose for special occasions / to celebrate her retirement from the college / a favorite restaurant / and the new life awaiting her / a half-hour drive from their home / a mountain town / twenty if she speeds in the thirty-mile zone / Tonight it makes more sense / a midway point / to arrive separately / as she will be driving down from her doctor's appointment / she gets there first / as he will be driving from home / he should have been there before her / she starts calling his cell / after waiting ten, twenty minutes / he doesn't answer / irritation turns to worry / no surprise there / always leaves it behind in his work-jeans pocket / the hospital, 911, the police / *Have you seen him?* / or turns off the sound at the movies and then forgets to turn it back on / *Can you please help me find him?* / Even now, months later / *about six feet, thinning hair, a boy's blue eyes* / when she knows good and well / dusk deepening / how he had been driving up the mountain / he feels a stab of pain / already thinking of what he might order / coming from his left side but radiating out / wondering about her state of mind / the special, if it is special / if she would be excited or terrified / or his default favorite, salmon with a lemon dill sauce / like a sword piercing his left side / substituting mashed potatoes for the fries—they're very good about substitutions / though how would he know what it feels like to have a sword piercing his left side? / because of his medical training understanding what is happening / not wanting to cause more harm / pronounced dead on arrival / he forgets to charge it and it runs out of juice / Even now, three months shy of a year later / pulling his car off the road, rolling gently to a stop / when she knows exactly what happened / a ditch that might as well be his grave / discovered by a passing cyclist, rushed to the ER / why he was late / a ruptured aortic aneurysm / as he is to be cremated and therefore have no grave, per se / neither he nor she could have foreseen / even now / *a boy's blue eyes* / and cannot comprehend how someone she loved / she keeps running and rerunning that night in her head / *Can you please help me find him?* / can be nothing but dust / unread emails, fragments, unpaid bills, memories / broken glass, dented bumper / a new life awaiting her / both terrified and excited / how can it be? / *Can you help me find him?* / a new life awaiting her / *Can you help me find him?* / a mystery she cannot by any means solve / nevertheless, she keeps asking / *Where are you?* / as this is the only way she knows / *Can you help me find him?* / how to create an afterlife for him /

ONE

Here there be dragons

Today, the magnet on her fridge proves pro-phetic: EVEN CREATURES OF HABIT CAN SOMETIMES BE FORGETFUL.

You said it, Antonia agrees. She has just poured orange juice into the coffee in the mug she brought back from one of the fancier hotels. Must have been a special occasion for Sam to have chosen to stay there and for her to have allowed the expense.

You'd think you were born with money in your family, she liked to tease him.

I never had it to begin with, so I'm not afraid to spend

it, Sam responded. He was always quick with a comeback. Used to get him in trouble with his dad growing up. Being fresh, it was called back then. Oh, the stories he told her.

Sam spoiled her, or tried to, and got scolded as his thanks—but it was the kind of scolding that must've made him suspect she liked being made something of.

There'll be no more of that now.

SHE IS KEEPING to her routines, walking a narrow path through the loss—not allowing her thoughts to stray. Occasionally, she takes sips of sorrow, afraid the big wave might wash her away. Widows leaping into a husband's pyre, mothers jumping into a child's grave. She has taught those stories.

Today, like every other day, you wake up empty and frightened, she quotes to herself as she looks at her reflection in the mirror in the morning. Her beloved Rumi no longer able to plug the holes.

Late afternoons as the day wanes, in bed in the middle of the night, in spite of her efforts, she finds herself at the outer edge where, in the old maps, the world drops off, and beyond is terra incognita, sea serpents, the Leviathan—HERE THERE BE DRAGONS.

Countless times a day, and night, she pulls herself

back from this edge. If not for herself, then for the others: her three sisters, a few old aunties, nieces and nephews. Her circle used to be wider. But she has had to pull in, contain the damage, keep breathing.

As she often tells her sister Izzy, always in crisis, arriving for visits with shopping bags full of gifts and a broken heart: the best thing you can give the people who love you is to take care of yourself so you don't become a burden on them. No wonder Izzy's ringtone for Antonia is church bells.

Actually, all the sisters have followed Izzy's lead and assigned that ringtone to Antonia. The secret got out. The secret always gets out in the sisterhood. Our Lady of Pronouncements, Mona said by way of explanation. Good old Mo-mo, no hairs on her tongue—one of their mother's Dominican sayings. Tilly was kinder. Sort of. It's because you started going to Sam's church. It's how Tilly used to describe their denomination, to avoid using the word *Christian*. Now she avoids Sam's name. *Your* church. As if Antonia would forget that Sam is gone unless someone reminds her.

They're just jealous, was Sam's theory about the ringtone profiling. All your years of teaching. You've picked up a lot of wisdom. A head full of chestnuts.

Full of B.S. That's what the sisterhood would say.

Who now to champion her way of being in the world?

She empties out the ruined coffee and starts over.

THE LITTLE PHONE she is carrying in her pocket begins ringing. She hasn't set special ringtones for anyone, except Mona, who insisted on dogs barking. Not just any dogs, but Mona's five rescues, which she set up on Antonia's phone.

Today it's Tilly calling. A few days ago, Mona. Izzy weaves in and out. The sisterhood checking in on her. You take her this morning. I'll call her this weekend. The frequency has dropped off the last few months, but it has been sweet.

How are you? they ask. How are you doing?

Come visit, they all say. Knowing she won't take them up on it. She is the sister who hates traveling even during the best of times.

It's beautiful here, Tilly brags. Why do you think it's called the *Heart*land? They have an ongoing rivalry. Vermont or Illinois. Who gets spring first, who has the worst snowfalls?

As she chats with her sister, Antonia hears plates clattering in the background. Tilly cannot abide being still. What are you doing? Antonia confronts her sister.

What do you mean what am I doing?

Those sounds.

What sounds?

How easily they slip into bickering. It's almost a relief when Tilly brings up Izzy. I'm worried, Tilly says. Izzy has been increasingly erratic. She is selling her house just outside of Boston, or not—they can't be sure. She is sleeping in friends' spare rooms or on their couches while she remodels her house.

But you're selling it, aren't you? the sisters try to reason with her.

It'll bring in more money if it's perfect.

Perfection takes time, not to mention money, which Izzy is always saying she doesn't have. Didn't she stop seeing her shrink because she said it was too much money? But you have insurance, don't you? The sisters again, the Dominican Greek chorus they become when some sister, usually Izzy, is headed for a downfall.

I don't want some insurance company knowing I'm going to a shrink. A shrink seeing a shrink! It would ruin my professional standing.

That bridge was burned a while back, according to Mona. Izzy is no longer at the mental health practice she helped start. Even master sleuth Mona isn't sure what all came down.

And she's also stopped the meds she was on, Tilly adds. Mona says you can't do that with those kind of meds. Tilly sighs, eerily still for a change, and then says, They had a huge fight. Those two, I tell you.

Antonia imagines Tilly shaking her head. It is odd that Izzy and Mona, the two therapists in the family, can't apply their professional skills to getting along. You said it, Antonia agrees, so as not to append something negative and quotable that will get back to the others, bring on more bickering.

Anyhow, sister, screw them. How are you doing?

I'm okay. Antonia's mantra of the last year. Somewhere she read that *okay* and *Coca-Cola* are the two most universally understood words. It depresses her to think the ties that bind are so flimsy. Even silence would be better.

But silence is all she gets when she addresses Sam these days. What she wouldn't give for his voice coming from the afterlife, assuring her that he's okay.

HER NEIGHBOR ROGER is at the door. If I can be of any help? he offers. Kind of late for that, she thinks. Sam's death was last June. Maybe the news just now reached him, like the light from stars?

I'm good, she tells Roger. A turn of phrase borrowed from her students. She always feels slightly bogus parroting them, as in her first years speaking English, tossing out an idiom, pretending she'd been born to it. *Dream on*. A phrase from her own student days.

Been hauling over to Ferrisburgh. Got to take what comes. Pays the bills anyhow. Roger is partial to sentence fragments; Antonia has to supply the rest. Every encounter, homework, a fill-in-the-blank test.

Broken English. The phrase once leveled at her and her sisters. She mended her broken pieces and ended up teaching Americans their own language, four decades total, three at the nearby college. What now, now that she has retired?

We shall see, her mother used to say. Que será, será.

Been meaning to stop. Them gutters—Roger nods at the pipe running the length of the house, right under the roof, full of twigs, leaves. Runoff from the roof, stuff collects.

I thought those were nests, Antonia says, laughing. Of course, she didn't really think so, but Roger gets such a kick out of knowing more than the smarty-pants professors over at the college. One of her ways of being neighborly. Letting him have the last word—it worked most times with Sam.

In fact, Antonia doesn't know how half the things in the house work. All state-of-the-art net-zero conservation systems Sam was so proud of. It's like flying a 747, she'd complain every time he tried to guide her through all the levers and dials in the furnace room.

And you call yourself a feminist! her sister Mona is quick to point out. Mona's default ringtone is sci-fi. The world is crazy, baby sister insists.

It's *The world is ugly, / And the people are sad*, Antonia is tempted to tell Mona, from a Stevens poem I used to teach. But it has never worked to treat her sisters like her students. I don't give a fuck who said so, Tilly has told her more than once.

I'll get them cleared up for you, Roger offers. A complete sentence, his way of being neighborly, instead of a sympathy card.

Later that morning, there's a knock at the door. Antonia checks the peephole, a new habit she's not likely to break since she is alone. She can just make out a head of glossy black hair. Mario, one of the Mexican workers next door. She opens to the boy-size man, his soft brown skin unusual in pale-faced Vermont. Rare also for Antonia to feel tall in this country. For a moment she understands the self-assurance of those who can look down at another's face. What comes with health care and good nutrition.

Mario doesn't look old enough to be doing the

milking next door. Roger might be breaking the child-labor laws. But then, he's got bigger problems, like the immigration status of his farmhands.

Hola, doñita. They've met before. Soon after his arrival early this year, Mario cut his hand on a saw he didn't know how to use. Lots of blood and Roger afraid to take him to the hospital, where the ER might call the ICE office. Instead, Roger called her. Didn't he know about Sam's death? I'm no doctor, she reminded her neighbor.

Not for the cut. To talk to him, calm him down, Roger explained. Small town. Everyone knows Dr. Sawyer's wife is Spanish.

Not really *Spanish Spanish*, she used to correct them. But she's given up trying to explain the colonial intricacies of her ethnicity. Soon after she and Sam married, one of his elderly patients stopped her at the grocery store to ask if he'd brought her back from one of his volunteer surgery trips, always written up in the local paper. Dr. Sawyer saving the world in Mexico, Panama, India, the Dominican, annoyingly shortening the name of her country. That, too, she's given up trying to correct.

Hola, Mario. ¿Qué pasa?

El patrón, Mario says, jerking his head toward the hardscrabble dairy farm next door. He says you need some help.

Sí, por favor. She comes out to stand in the driveway. The ladder is already leaning against the side of the house. No car or pickup in sight. She didn't hear a motor. Did he carry it across the pasture? It must be three times his height. Gutters, she says, pointing to the roof. She uses the English word, not out of any instructional motive, but because she doesn't know the word for *rain gutter* in Spanish.

They have to be cleaned out, she explains. My husband, he used to do it. She can't bring herself to pronounce Sam dead.

Mario takes off his cap, holds it to his heart. Mis sentimientos, doñita.

Antonia's eyes well up. Somehow it gets to her more when the condolences are in Spanish. The roots go deeper. Small sips, she reminds herself, and nods up at the gutter. Thank you for your help. Call me when you are done, okay? She means to pay him for his trouble.

Okay, he says, that universal word. But instead of turning to the job at hand, he keeps standing before her, perhaps searching for another universal word.

Anything else you need, Mario?

Bueno, doñita, Mario hesitates, flashing her a megawatt smile—too bad about the teeth. Same back home in the DR, the poor with missing molars, rotted stubs. All that processed sugar. Everyone drinking Coca-Cola instead of the natural juices from the tropical fruits that abound. Yes, Mona, *The world is ugly, / And the people are sad*. Her mind is full of quotations, the slate never wiped clean, always the feeling that she is plagiarizing someone else's wisdom.

Mario does have a favor to ask. Maybe when he has finished, la doñita can help him call his girlfriend?

Antonia feels the flicker of irritation. Isn't she entitled to a grace period after a loss? She has no energy for extras. *Duelo*, they call it in Spanish: bruised and hurting all over. Mario, of all people, should know. In their cultures, a person in duelo is left alone.

In need there is no season, Sam would say. Reluctantly, she tells the young man okay.

Mario has one more question. Where will the birds lay their eggs now, doñita?

It takes her a moment to understand. It's not a nest, she explains. Basura, trash. A nest requires intention. The difference between a home and a shelter. What is her house with Sam gone? A home, a shelter? She wishes she still had her students to ask. She is alone now with her intense need to get the words right.

SHE WATCHES HIM all morning from one window, then another. Maybe he's taking his time to avoid getting back to his farm work. Or maybe he's calculating, so as to finish just when it'll be the right time to call his girlfriend in Mexico. Mi novia, he had said. More than a girlfriend. A bride, a fiancée. What time is it in Mexico now?

She is not policing him so much as making sure that he doesn't fall. And if he does, then what? Does she call 911 for help? Take him to the hospital? Better the Open Door Clinic, if they are open, where the staff, mostly volunteers, are poor-friendly, undocumented-friendly, friendly period. Before Sam's death, she used to volunteer there, translating for the migrant workers. Of course, anything serious, the clinic would send him over to the hospital, where they're more fearful of liabilities. They might notify the sheriff, who'd come racing over to the ER, sirens going, lights flashing. Or they'd ask if he has insurance, as he lies on a gurney, bleeding to death. Who is allowed to have access to care? Universal health care, Sam argued. He could ruin a dinner party with his fierce advocacy. How can we call ourselves civilized and withhold care from those who can't afford it? He was invited on several local talk shows and college panels. Some of his colleagues at the hospital began shunning him. But the younger doctors, especially the young women, regarded him as their mentor.

Of course, Antonia agreed with Sam, though she let him do the arguing. Even now, long after immigrating as a child, she still thinks of it as "their" country. Not for her to meddle in their affairs. Besides, Sam was better at arguing, sticking to the topic, not getting teary and tongue-tied when someone disputed her facts. Over the years, there was so much overlap in their opinions. She could tell what he thought from a glance at his face, the tone of his voice as he spoke on the phone in another room. Nice to get to that place with someone where you don't have to ask. A different kind of silence now. She has the radio going constantly. She makes a mental note to up her contribution to VPR during the next membership drive.

SHE'S OUT COLLECTING the mail when she spots the sheriff's car coming slowly down the road toward her house. Instantly, she is alert, some instinctive reaction, like seeing a hornet in her vicinity. She runs down a checklist. What could she be doing wrong? On the top of the list would be the small brown undocumented man cleaning her gutters. But Mario has finally made it to the back of the house. Antonia lifts a hand casually in greeting, a performed rather than an innocent gesture. *One may smile, and smile, and be a villain.* Would the sheriff recognize *Hamlet*? Most of the law enforcement in town are local boys whose family farms have gone under. Many didn't even finish high school, thinking they'd end up farming. Besides, as

Sam often reminded her with a bemused chuckle: not everyone in the world walks around with a whole bunch of famous people talking to them in their heads.

Once she's inside, she hurries toward the back of the house, sliding open the glass door off the living room. Ven, ven, she calls out. Rápido, rápido! La migra! she adds to hurry him. It works. Mario scrambles down from the ladder, missing a rung, and bounds toward her, still clutching a fistful of leaves.

She hurries him inside, points to a chair in the corner, out of view of any windows. *Harboring a fugitive*, the phrase runs through her head. What Sam would have done, unquestioningly. He was the bold one. She, the reluctant activist, though everyone assumed it was she who was the political one by virtue of her ethnicity, as if being Latina automatically conferred a certain radical stance.

Mario glances around the room wildly. Does he think Antonia has laid a trap for him? There's a knocking at the door. Who could it be? Stay here, tranquilo, away from the windows. In the driveway, the UPS truck is already pulling away. The book she ordered that's supposed to help with grief lies on the welcome mat. Antonia checks the road again: the sheriff's car has stopped at Roger's. Good thing Mario's here. But then there's José, Mario's co-worker, perhaps cleaning stalls or mixing the feed, or if he's on break, napping or listening to his tapes of Mexican music in the trailer behind the farmhouse.

As Antonia watches, the sheriff gets back in his cruiser and heads down the road, turning right at the corner, toward the rumbly bridge, where there's a pull-off. Time for his lunch, riding beside him in a cooler, or maybe he's meeting someone he can't invite home. Antonia has heard he's divorced, living with his mother.

Years ago, Mona talked her and Sam into making an annual donation to their local sheriff's fund. They send you a sticker, Mona explained. You put it on your car window. You'll never get a ticket again, I swear.

Smart cookie, baby sister Mo-mo. But Sam was doubtful. Another one of your sister's theories. Let's try it for a year, Antonia persuaded him. Against his better judgment, he had affixed the sticker to their Subaru.

That was over five years ago. They haven't gotten a ticket since.

Other people are sometimes right, she reminded him. Other people, meaning her sisters, herself.

I never said they weren't. He was too damn quick with his comebacks, right even about not always being right.

ROGER COMES TO collect Mario. What's he doing? Putting on a new roof or what?

She takes the blame. She had him come inside. Sheriff was on the prowl.

Came by my place, too, asking how things were going. Somebody's talking. Roger looks at her pointedly, so she feels she has to deny that she has spoken to anyone. Why would she endanger one of her own?

Roger shrugs. A shrug that implicates her whole gender. Women. Always talking. They talk when they're having their hair done; they talk waiting on line at the grocery store; they talk when they stop by to pick up their Thanksgiving turkeys from Roger's honor store.

He's in the living room, Antonia says, stepping to one side for Roger to come in, casting a look at his dirty boots. She considers asking him to remove them, as he seems to have missed the hint of shoes lined up below the mudroom pegs. But she might as well ask him to take off his clothes. No way this old Vermonter's going to walk around in stocking feet indoors.

Mario is not in the living room where she left him, but there's a fistful of leaves piled on the seat of the chair in the corner.

Mario! she calls. Es el patrón. To Roger, she says, he probably got scared. I told him it was la migra.

Roger lets out an audible sigh. Women overreacting. Mario! he calls in a commanding voice. They hear footsteps coming down the hall. Someone else who didn't remove his shoes. But what unsettles her is that Mario took the liberty of hiding in the bedroom wing, a private part of the house.

Took the liberty? Sam would have challenged her. What does that even mean, when you are facing deportation?

Me agarró el temor, Mario says. Grabbed by fear. Personification is not merely a literary term, she used to tell her classes. Literature has to pull its weight in the real world or else it's of no use to us. It's not just Sam at dinner parties who could get in high dudgeon. Mario is holding himself, presumably to stop shaking. The red string bracelet he wears as a talisman on his left hand dangles its two loose ends. Suerte y protección, he had explained, wincing as she bandaged his hand. A lot of good it did you, she thought but didn't say, concentrating on administering the first aid she'd picked up from Sam over the years. She had felt such tenderness then, and now again, at this boy-man who believes he can tame the dragons with a piece of braided string. No different from her literary cache of salutary lines. Tranquilo, tranquilo, she calms him. Estamos en Vermont. Here there be no torture of prisoners. He stares back, unconvinced. The world is crazy. Who knows what angry people will do.

Maybe you should wait a while before you take him back, Antonia advises. If you can spare him a little longer, I could use his help with a few things. Windows to wash. Lawn furniture to haul out of the shed. She makes up a list of improvised chores to delay his return. Best not to mention the promised phone call.

Roger scowls, looking them both over, probably suspecting they're up to something. Okay, but I need the ladder back. Roger heads out the front door, and moments later his pickup pulls into the backyard, where she and Mario are waiting. After the two men load the ladder, Roger points to his left wrist, where he'd wear a watch if he wore such things. Be back by the afternoon milking.

Sí, patrón, sí, Mario answers, in a voice so submissive it pains Antonia to hear it.

Roger drives away, the ladder poking out the back of the lowered flatbed. Antonia notes the red plastic ribbon tied to one end to alert cars to keep their distance.

MARIO PULLS OUT a wallet from his back pocket. Monogrammed RL, Ralph Lauren? A fancy brand for a poor man, but then most of these brands are now pirated, cheap imitations sold on city streets by migrants in stocking caps, calling her over in accents from Haiti, Mexico, Ethiopia, countries she isn't sure where they are on the map. Burkina Faso was the last one that took her by surprise. Remind me where it is, she had asked Sam, as if she had only momentarily forgotten. She didn't want him teasing her about one more deficiency of her Dominican primary school education, adding her poor sense of geography to her deplorable math skills. He wouldn't let her reconcile their checkbook.

Tucked inside the sleeve of Mario's wallet is a worn piece of paper. Soon it will disintegrate with all the unfolding, refolding. Mario holds it out to her. *Estela*, written in a rough hand, then an area code and phone number. That's all? she asks, and he nods. I thought for Mexico you needed more? Yes, you do, but she is not in Mexico. She is in Colorado. The way he pronounces the name, it sounds like a state in Mexico. But no, his novia has already crossed over. Estela has encountered some problem with being released. The coyotes have refused to put her on a bus to Burlington.

A bus cross-country by herself? Antonia questions. Does she speak English? Does she have her passport? What if she's apprehended? Furthermore, does la novia have her parents' consent? Does el patrón know?

La novia does not speak English. She has no pasaporte. She has only her mother and little sisters, the father died, no brothers to protect her. The coyotes would bring her door-to-door for more money than Mario has. Many have made the journey safely by bus. Mario answers every one of la doñita's questions readily. But then he comes to a full stop. Here be his dragon: el patrón. Señor Roger is a hard man, Mario offers, watching to see if Antonia will agree before he goes on to admit that el patrón does not know Mario's girlfriend will be arriving at his doorstep to live with him.

Antonia looks back at the young face, the high cheekbones, the carved features. Eighteen, he's told her, no older than her first-years at the college. But although he has the slender body of a boy, Mario's eyes are those of an old soul, the brown iris almost filling the socket, only a thin white rim showing, like the sun right before a full eclipse. If she continues to stare at them, will she go blind? And small as he is, Mario could kill her, cut her throat. The disquieting thought surprises her. More and more in her post-Sam life, things previously not dangerous now seem potentially so. No wonder all religions urge followers to care for the widow. Widow. What a name. Girlfriend, novia, esposa, viuda.

And when are you planning to tell el patrón?

Mario bows his head like a penitent boy. Maybe la doñita can help him with this?

Why would el patrón listen to me? I don't know him. We're just neighbors. Antonia can hear her mother's scolding voice coming out of her mouth. She doesn't want to berate him. He's worried enough. But she can't seem to help herself, some bully impulse to keep swinging even when your victim is down. And if I ask el patrón, and he says no, what are you going to do then, eh?

Mario doesn't have to reply; what he is thinking is written all over his face. He now has seen the wing with its three bedrooms: her study, the master bedroom, and a guest room. Perhaps that's what he was doing by taking the liberty? Checking out the accommodations for the girlfriend.

Anything else you need? she made the mistake of asking. In a similar situation, wouldn't anyone ask as much? A Sam question. If there were any dinner parties coming up— not the obligation suppers friends and acquaintances have been inviting her to, but a freewheeling dinner party with sparkling conversation—she would bring up the question. Who do we ask for help when we've run out of options?

She hands the phone to Mario, then exits the room, not only out of respect for their privacy. She cannot bear to hear the happy voices of lovers reconnecting.

DOÑITA, MARIO CALLS, toward the bedroom wing where she has disappeared. Mi novia quiere darle las gracias.

Thank her for what? Antonia hasn't agreed to anything. But how can she refuse just talking to the girl? What is the minimum one owes another? Another dinner-party question.

Doñita, muchísimas gracias. The girl sounds timid, scared, her voice just above a whisper. And yet she has been gutsy enough to make the perilous journey north from the southern tip of Mexico—where Mario has told her he is from—the whole length of the country, over the border, through the desert, braving la migra, dubious smugglers, fellow travelers. All the dragons.

Gracias, gracias, the girl keeps saying. Her gratitude is hard to bear. De nada, Antonia replies, a more accurate rejoinder than *you're welcome*: she has done nothing to be thanked for.

SHE CONSIDERS SENDING Mario back on foot, across the back pasture, by the tree line, safely out of sight of the road. This might give him the message that she is not available for further favors: making arrangements for the bus ticket, picking up Estela in Burlington, getting her some warm clothes.

But Antonia cedes, as she always did with Sam, the good cop, who seems to be resurrecting inside her. A part of you dies with them, Antonia now knows, but wait awhile, and they return, bringing you back with them. So, is this all his afterlife will amount to? Sam-inspired deeds from the people who loved him?

She drives Mario home, and once there, decides to get it over and done with. She knocks at Roger's back door, as she has never seen anyone come in or go out the front door in her thirty years on this road. When he doesn't answer, Antonia is relieved. She has done her part.

Mario is waiting for her beside the car. He looks relieved as well. Maybe it is best if la doñita talks to el patrón after the girlfriend arrives?

And where will you put her if he says no? Antonia asks crossly.

Just then, Roger comes out from the barn, looking annoyed, too. Maybe he's had an altercation with one of his cows or an old piece of machinery quit or José broke it—or does Roger even need a reason? Seems he's always cranky. The old Vermonter. Makes it easier when you can pin someone down as a type with a ringtone or label. What type would Sam be? *Have been*, she corrects herself. And she? The bereft widow? The whiny widow? The wise widow? What kind of widow does she want to be?

Before she's done conveying Mario's request, Roger is shaking his head. No, he says, n-o, same word in Spanish as in English. He glares at Mario, who takes a step back as if the fire keeping him warm has suddenly flared up.

Got enough trouble with the two of them. He better start packing.

She doesn't have to translate for Mario. It's quite clear what Roger is saying. A hard man, el patrón, Mario said so himself.

But the girl is already on her way, Antonia pleads.

That's his problem, Roger says, red-faced. I didn't give you permission, he hollers at the cowering Mario. His nostrils flare, he lurches forward, his forehead lowered like a bull going after the red cape. It occurs to Antonia how much certain people remind her of animals. If he doesn't calm down, Roger might end up with a heart attack. What if Antonia has to drive him over to the ER? When did life become so fraught? Pre or post Sam's passing?

Roger stomps off toward the trailer. What's he planning to do? Throw all of Mario's things out in the yard?

Tell el patrón that I will find her another accommodation. Mario pleads. Por favor.

Roger! Antonia calls, and when he doesn't stop, she runs after him. Mario will find her another place.

Roger swivels on the spot, taking Antonia's measure, in case she has a trick up her sleeve. Where's he going to put her? Your house?

It's Antonia's turn to shake her head. I can't handle something like this right now. I've got enough troubles.

Roger stares back at her, his eyes small and mean in their puffy eye sockets, like the eyes of the pigs he fattens and slaughters and sells at his honor store. People drive out from town to buy his bacon and pork chops, his Thanksgiving turkeys, the fresh eggs he's not allowed to say are organic because he'd have to pay some company to investigate and certify it is so.

You're the ones always saying everybody's welcome. Roger points at Antonia. He must mean Sam. A few years back Roger posted a sign by his mailbox, TAKE BACK VERMONT. No use pointing out the irony: he's now hiring Mexicans. People can be full of paradoxes when their own pockets are affected. Sam retaliated with his own, TAKE VERMONT FORWARD. Needless to say, the two neighbors did not see eye to eye.

Dr. Sawyer always was the bleeding heart, Roger indicts Sam now.

Antonia feels the anger rising inside her. The man has no delicacy. Maybe no one's told him that Sam died of an aortic aneurysm? In spite of her efforts, the big wave

hits, the anger turns to tears, soul-gouging sobs of someone who has been holding back her sadness, her fears
for months. Both Roger and Mario come to her, one at
each arm, as if she is too weak to hold herself up.

No need to start bawling, the farmer says gruffly.
The girlfriend can stay, a week tops. Just a week, he
adds, when her face lights up with relief. He scowls with
the exertion of drawing this kindness out from deep
inside him. A miracle that these feelings persist in his
hard heart. Goes to show, she or Sam would have later
commented to each other. Roger's not as much a type as
we thought.

We shall see. Que será, será. Mami again. Will all the
dead be resurrecting now?

BACK AT THE HOUSE, there's a message on her machine.
Doñita, por favor, dígale a Mario que el coyote quiere
mas dinero para soltarme. The girl's voice is shaky. Then
a man is shouting. You want us to release your girl, you
better wire what you owe.

Antonia keeps dialing the number, but no one picks
up.

What now? Does she drive back over and tell Mario?
Didn't he say he was all paid up except for the bus
ticket? Maybe the coyotes are pissed Mario didn't buy

the door-to-door package? Who knows? Mario, Estela, José—they are all residents of dragon country, no man's land beyond the gated communities of belonging.

Let sleeping dogs lie for now. Antonia has done all she can. But as she gets into bed, she feels unsettled as well as irritated, above all else with Sam for leaving her alone to do justice to the things they believed in.

You want me to be a better person, then come back and help me out, she addresses the darkness of their bedroom. She watches with hawk eyes for the slightest sign of some kind. The air circulator hums awake. The outdoor floodlights flash on—she can see the glow from her bedroom window. Sam had those movement lights installed, thinking they'd deter deer from getting in his garden. Trigger-happy, they turn on if a squirrel darts by. If the wind is coming strong from the north. Drives her batty. Worrying each time that it might be an intruder. And now, especially. Out in the fields surrounding her house, the coydogs have started up their howling, a haunting sound, but not otherworldly, just a part of the natural world.

Anything else you need? she had asked Mario, a throwaway question in the circles she runs in, but in some parts of the world, among the neediest, what has been thrown away elsewhere gets recycled, put to good use. The lights flash on again and again, then fade away. Tomorrow, which is already today, she will call the electrician who installed them to have them taken down. She wants outdoor lights she can turn off and on. The world is a crazy place. But she doesn't need to be alerted each time a dragon comes close.

TWO

Where is Burkina Faso?

She waits until a light comes on in the trailer, Mario and José getting up for the first milking of the day. And to think: this happens before dawn every morning, with or without her insomnia to note it.

Wouldn't it make a great book? She had mentioned it several times to Sam. Short chapters about the people who keep our world going? Invisible people we don't even know about?

Invisible to whom? Sam had a way of asking questions that always stopped her short.

It would make a great book, Sam agreed once she explained.

Antonia has a pile of these ideas in a shoebox she used to keep in her office at the college. For students who said they had nothing to write about. Here, pick one, she'd offer. She misses them, her access to the young. Another downside to being childless, which, she read recently, is no longer the politically correct term. *Nonparent* carries no judgment. *Childless mother*, a former colleague called herself. Maybe others share her intense need to get the words right. But what if their right words sound wrong to her?

Is this what happens to an imagination in old age, a bag lady of great ideas, a snapped necklace, the beads scattering? Years later, she finds the odd trinket: a shiny blue bead with a hole through it. Where did it come from? A lost piece that has left something else incomplete. Along with the shoebox, Antonia has a tin for such findings. Years from now, the item it was a part of will surface, and she will supply the missing bit, making the thing whole again.

Could that possibly be what the afterlife amounts to: an eternity of re-memberings? Over to you, Sam. She talks to him in her head. You always liked being the one to know. But the afterlife has changed him. He no longer seems interested in having the last word.

* * *

SHE DECIDES TO walk over to her neighbor's. If she drives, Roger will hear the car, come out, ask questions. He gets a whiff of any trouble and he'll rescind the week of grace. Last time there were rumors of raids on Vermont farms, Roger dismissed his workers. Mario and José are recent hires. Antonia has no idea where their predecessors went. Now that she has stopped volunteering, she's no longer in the migrant gossip loop. Maybe Roger's former workers went to another patrón in Vermont? To Canada? Maybe back to Mexico? Everybody knows not to build a house on shifting sand. Good for temporary shelters, but a home needs a foundation.

It's still dark. The sun is not yet up. The road is deserted; tall pines on either side make for creepy stretches. In a few hours, the sky will flood with that early-spring watercolor light that can bring tears to her eyes. The road will get busy with what passes for busy on a dirt road in backcountry Vermont: the school bus whose driver waves by lifting a finger; the newspaper delivery man who she has heard has a terrible stutter—she wouldn't know, she has never spoken to him; the garbage truck driven by a guy with a shaved head, a leering look, who slows down, then floors the gas, probably in disappointment that the little lady turns out to be a little old lady. All these lives that are not her life. Bless them all, she thinks, even the garbage guy—before she can think again that she has no credentials for blessing anyone.

It's chilly. She quickens her steps. In a break in the trees, she sees a few stars still shining. Have you ever noticed how the stars are brightest on the coldest nights?

You always say that, Sam would say, chuckling.

Remind me again, where is Burkina Faso?

That made him chuckle, too. It became their code phrase. A way of reminding each other to stay humble, as there would always be things they didn't know.

THE WALK IS INVIGORATING. Maybe she'll do this every morning. Instead of yoga. Take a walk. "Weather permitting," Vermonters' version of *si Dios quiere*. She'll be one of those invisible people in the book she will never write. Not that she is doing anything useful to keep the world going. Except to keep herself going. The best thing she can do for the people she loves is to take care of herself. But what if that person she loves the most no longer needs her stoicism?

Her mind flashes back to the troubling talk with Tilly about Izzy—was it only yesterday? She wonders about Mona's diagnosis that their sister is seriously ill. But then Mona is always diagnosing everyone—a professional handicap for a therapist, much like quoting is for Antonia, the teacher. Izzy is just being Izzy. Sure she's made some poor choices, but then haven't they all?

She's used up all her savings, Tilly reported hearing through the grapevine. No, Tilly can't say who told her. (Easy to do the math on that one: not Antonia, couldn't be Izzy telling on herself, ergo Mona.)

Savings? Antonia challenged. Izzy has savings? That's a total oxymoron.

Tilly's feathers were ruffled. Who are you calling a moron?

She's always saying she's broke.

Well she gave a pile of money to that guy in Cuba—

Wait! She was in Cuba?

See what I mean? Tilly says triumphantly.

She's having a good time anyhow, Antonia defended their sister. But was Izzy really enjoying herself? And what was going to happen when Izzy reached old age having burned every bridge to safety and solvency? Antonia knows what Izzy would say. How do you think most of the world's viejitos live—if they even get to be old?

She recalls Mario talking about his frail mother, pobrecita, getting so old. She can't walk anywhere anymore. How old is your mother? Antonia had asked. Cincuenta y cuatro. Fifty-four! Do you know how old I am, Mario? The young man didn't dare a guess. No

puede ser, doñita, he exclaimed when she told him.
Sesenta y cinco! Of course, one has to factor in other
variables. Just as a year in the life of a dog is equivalent
to seven human ones—so she has heard from Mona, the
dog lover—poverty years have to be more aging than
affluent ones.

How does the imagination of the poor age? Perhaps
from much practice over the course of a lifetime—
always having to imagine a better life—it stays vigor-
ous. At a recent reading at the college, a guest lecturer
spoke about the origins of Black English. This rich folk
language is what occurred when African people with
an intensely musical and oral culture came up against
the King James Bible and the sweet-talking American
South, under conditions that denied them all outlets for
their visions and gifts except the transformation of the
English language into song.

So are songs and stories what we come to when we
are divested of all other protections and privileges? *These
fragments I have shored against my ruins*? *The Waste
Land* was always a favorite with her students, many
of whom had known only plentitude. And what about
those who cannot bear up under deprivations, who are
traumatized and silenced by hard times? If she ever gets
back to writing, Antonia wants the stories she tells—like

the writers she depends on—to come from that deeper, hurting place. Perhaps grief will be good for her work?

If so, thanks, but no thanks. Once again she is talking to Sam as if he has offered her this consolation for his absence.

WHEN NO ONE answers her knock at the trailer, Antonia heads for the barn, where she finds Mario shoveling fresh sawdust from a wheelbarrow into each stall. In the milking parlor, José is manning the machines, softly cursing at the cows.

Antonia remembers overhearing some farmers who had brought in their workers at the Open Door Clinic. She'd been called in to translate that night. Both the hospital and the clinic were seeing an increase in Spanish-speaking cases, but unlike the hospital, the clinic couldn't afford off-site interpreting services. The farmers were talking among themselves about how they preferred women milkers to men. Antonia had dismissed them as sexist comments, until she realized their point was that the women were gentler with the animals. The cows actually give more milk. The little calves thrive.

Psst! Mario! She calls to him, startling him. Is el patrón around? He shakes his head.

Your novia called again. The coyotes are threatening

her. Who are these people you hired? she asks, as if Mario should have checked references first, done his due diligence.

Ay, doñita, ay. The young man clutches his head. What is he to do? The coyotes are insisting on the drop-off fee to Burlington even if they put la novia on a bus in Denver. He has sent those chingados all the savings he had, borrowed the rest. The paisanos all pitched in. That's how they work it. First, I bring my novia or wife or sister or little brother with your help. Then I help you bring yours. Slowly and all together, we rebuild our lives here. A nest, a home, not just a trailer on shifting sand.

I tried to call back but no answer. Come over and we'll try again when you're done with the milking. Otherwise, el patrón . . . No need to complete the sentence. They both know what she means.

Sí, sí, sí, doñita. Mario's face is lined with worry. She has a sudden glimpse of what he will look like when he is an old man of fifty-four.

BACK AT HER HOUSE, she lies down, hoping to go back to sleep until Mario arrives. But she is too worked up. She's going to have to call Vivian and Franklin and cancel. No way she can attend a dinner party tonight on no sleep in her state of mind.

If her sisters are indeed taking turns, Mona will be calling today. She'll have the latest on Izzy. Or who knows, maybe wild-card Izzy will phone in herself, wanting to know about Antonia's plans for her birthday this weekend. They will have heard through the sister grapevine that Antonia turned down Tilly's invitation to come celebrate it in Chicago. But Antonia is suddenly reconsidering. By leaving town, she will be released from this mess that has come to her door, dragons crawling ashore.

Since she can't sleep, she might as well do her morning meditation lying down in bed. The Buddha would not approve. But wait, the Buddha wouldn't care. The start-up gong on her phone meditation app sounds; in twenty minutes it will sound again, startling her in her woolgathering, her brain turning over and over the last twenty-four hours: Izzy and how to help her, the gutters filled with leaves and twigs, Mario calling Estela from her phone . . . her mind suddenly snags on that detail. Why does Mario need to come here to call Estela? Doesn't he have his own phone? Every undocumented worker she has met has a cell phone. Their one connection to home. Why does Mario need to involve her?

As if in answer to her question, the landline rings. It's not yet seven. Too early for one of her sisters. It's Roger. He doesn't bother to introduce himself or offer any of the niceties of good morning, how are you, hope I didn't wake you. He launches right in: Does Antonia need Mario's help today? She mentioned some window washing? If so, Roger can drop off the ladder on his way to town, pick it up later as he won't be needing it today. No niceties, but who cares? It's awful nice of you, Antonia thanks him.

A few minutes later, his pickup turns into her driveway then heads down to the back of the house. She hears him unloading the ladder—presumably by himself. Easier unloading than loading it. Sounds like a rule of life, she would have noted to Sam. She loved it when ordinary observations or a string of simple words suddenly opened up to reveal some profundity. You don't say, Sam would often respond to her insights. She was never sure what to make of that expression. It was one more of those Americanisms that would sometimes ambush her, and she would feel all over again that there was some deep core in English that she couldn't access.

WHEN HE SHOWS UP, Mario has already called around. On what phone? she confronts him, startling him. José's and mine, doñita. They bought it together. But they don't have a plan. No permanent address where the bills can be sent, no credit card, no credit. They buy phone cards,

save up their minutes for calling Mexico. And knowing English, la doñita could help in making any travel
arrangements.

Mario goes on to report that his paisanos have all
agreed to help. To the tune of several hundred more.
There is only so much they can spare. Everyone has to
budget. Antonia calls the Colorado number but hands
the phone over and leaves Mario to his negotiations. She
is not getting in any deeper. She has decided. This weekend, for her birthday, she'll be in Chicago.

In her bedroom, Antonia phones Vivian on her cell,
too late remembering it is too early. But Vivian is already
up. Really looking forward to tonight. We also invited
Wendy and poor Jim Blake. Does Vivian refer to her as
poor Antonia when talking to Wendy and Jim Blake?

How to wiggle out of it now? Antonia could plead
illness, but then Vivian will insist on coming over. A dinner party you can leave early, but a friend at your door
with a container of bean salad and a plate of brownies is
harder to get rid of. She could tell Vivian the truth: I'm
overwhelmed, didn't sleep last night or the night before
or the night before. No, it's not just grief, it's me. She
read the book her therapist recommended, *The Highly
Sensitive Person*. She found it in the college's science
library, which gave the book a certain legitimacy, not

just a feel-good self-help flash in the social-science pan. The author outlined how certain organisms are highly reactive, get easily overwhelmed, require a different eco-system to thrive. Not a pathology, a type. It was reassuring to read the book. An earlier patron had marked it up, inked notes in the margins, passages underlined, highlighted—in a library book, imagine! A highly sensitive person overreacting.

So, how are you? Vivian wants to know, her voice tinged with concern.

I'm okay, Antonia replies, a tad too quickly to be totally convincing. But Vivian doesn't probe further. The landscape of grief is not very inviting. Visitors don't want to linger. The best thing you can do for the people who love you is to usher them quickly through it. She does not want to become "poor Antonia."

Thanks for asking, Antonia says, closing the subject. This would be the moment to say she won't be coming tonight. But Antonia can't bring herself to do it, bailing out of a dinner party she knows damn well has been assembled to support her.

She and Franklin are so looking forward to tonight, Vivian says brightly. Antonia doubts Franklin is look-ing forward to all of his wife's poor friends at his table. Franklin never says much, until a remark triggers him and he is launched. The discovery of gravity waves. The inaccuracies of historical fiction. Solar eclipses and how long they will have to wait until the next one. (This one she has heard several times and she still can't seem to remember how long.) The wines of Chile.

And here she used to worry about Sam going on and on about universal health care. At least Sam only had one bone to pick in public. But maybe diversity is better if you're going to be a bore.

Just checking in. What time tonight and what can I bring?

Six-ish? And not a thing, just yourself.

When people say not to bring something, do you still bring wine? When they add *-ish* to the hour, when do they really want you at their door? She should know these things, as she and Sam often had people over. Will she be entertaining now that she is alone? She misses it, guests around the table, chili made with ground beef from Roger's honor store, cornbread made with Sam's blue corn.

BACK IN THE LIVING ROOM, Mario is standing at the window looking down at the ladder.

He sighs in response to her questions. El coyote requires three hundred more dollars just to release

Estela. Mario can cover that amount with what he has borrowed. But he also has to come up with the money for Estela's bus ticket to Burlington.

They're using you, Antonia fumes, shaking her head at Mario. They'll never be satisfied.

Puede ser, Mario nods. But what choice does he have but to keep the one he loves safe? What would you do if it were you, doñita?

She should take him to tonight's dinner party. Poor Mario has a question for our group.

She knows what her friend Vivian would do. Vivian supports worthy causes, just as she does her poor friends. She would write a check. No questions asked. But then Vivian can afford casting her bread upon the waters. She married the bakery owner, so to speak. Franklin's surname is a famous brand name. Yes, that family. He doesn't have to work for a living, which is why he went into teaching, he explained at one dinner party. Didn't even register that there were teachers present, the kind who needed to work to pay their property taxes, health insurance, their kids' college tuitions.

Ay, doñita querida, Mario says, in the cajoling voice of a young man flirting with an older woman. He knows it is a lot to ask—but would Antonia be willing to loan him the money to buy the bus ticket? *Loan*, a way for the poor back home to save face. A loan, not a handout, which the gracious and generous always forgive.

She gives him a nod of consideration, not a yes, but not a no. Highly sensitive people need time and quiet as they are easily overwhelmed, especially when they are grieving. Who is she kidding? She has already decided. Of course, she will buy Estela's bus ticket, but she will make the arrangements herself to ensure the money goes where it should go. The charitable gesture, hemmed in by suspicion. Not Izzy's way or Sam's. Sam, who got taken left and right, so that she always had to be the vigilant one, the bad cop. Don't you think I'd like to indulge myself for once, she complained to him. Be my guest, he said. Why not two good cops?

Mario is beside himself with gratitude. He grabs her hands, kisses them, a nearly extinct gesture only seen these days on stage, Shakespearean plays at the college, and in telenovelas.

¡Ya, ya, ya! she says, dismissing his lavish response. She knows what she has been thinking. Thank God people can't see inside each other's heads.

While he waits beside her, she checks online for tickets. Several options are available. The northern route goes through Toronto, then drops back down to Vermont. Best not to cross an international border with no passport or papers. The southern route is better, but it will involve a number of transfers. Estela might have trouble finding her way. Maybe Greyhound has a service? How does Antonia find out? Call the 800 number and ask the rep if they can help transfer an undocumented person from one bus to another? She notes the different time options. Meanwhile, Mario is to let her know when he has wired the money to the coyote, so Antonia can finish booking the ticket for Estela to pick up at the station in Denver. Mario provides all of Estela's information. The full name. Estela Adelia Cruz Fuentes. For home address and number, Antonia will have to use her own. God forbid Greyhound should contact Roger.

When they are done, Mario again grabs her hands. Ya, ya, she stops him. He must not confuse her with a truly good person—a truly good person would not feel relieved about hightailing it to Chicago and leaving these kids in the lurch. But how much can one person take on? We live in America, she reminds the disapproving Sam in her head, where you put your oxygen mask on first.

But either way, the plane is going to crash. So why not tender a little kindness before she, too, is a body in a ditch on the side of the road, availing herself of whatever afterlife will be afforded in somebody else's head, if that? Unlike Sam, who can enjoy his afterlife romping through her head, Antonia will not have Sam to keep her alive in his imagination.

On the ride back to Roger's with Mario, Antonia sees the sheriff's car in her rearview. Very calmly, as if she were speaking to a highly sensitive person, Antonia tells Mario la policía is behind them. He is to slide down in his seat. Clear the window. Mario does as he is told. She turns on her blinker to go into Roger's driveway, the cautious widow making a breakfast purchase at the honor store. The cruiser goes by, someone is riding with the sheriff, someone with disarmingly blonde, shoulder-length hair. The sheriff does not wave or look over her way.

ANTONIA CALLS IZZY purportedly to report on her plans for her birthday. Mostly, she wants to gauge her sister's state of mind for herself. Too often in their family, things are blown out of proportion. Was it growing up in a dictatorship that skewed their temperaments toward doom and gloom?

Izzy is full of news about her own plans. You know that Latino arts center I told you about? I found the perfect place. Western Mass! It'll be a way of importing diversity into that part of the state, a model to be copied throughout other white-bread areas of the country. Instead of migrant workers on farms, a cultural takeover: migrant poets, dancers, and artists. Would Antonia agree to be on the board, convince some of her writer friends to join?

Izzy, honey, how are you going to pay for all this?

We'll burn that bridge when we come to it, Izzy proclaims. (Precisely what she would do, Antonia thinks.) For starters, maybe Antonia's publisher is interested in putting together an anthology of their stories, profits to go to—

Antonia cuts her off. Izzy, honey, I haven't been in touch with my publisher forever. I'm really not up to it right now.

It'd be a way for you to get back in the saddle, Izzy says in her older-sister voice. Anyhow, think about it, okay? Izzy's actually headed to Western Mass now. Would Antonia like to join her for her birthday?

I'm going to Tilly's, Antonia's decision is now definite. I just bought my ticket. A little white lie. Antonia has a stash of them locked away in that closet of half-truths she has told the sisters over the years to avoid their disappointment, ire, or worse.

But I heard you didn't want to go anywhere for your birthday. What made you change your mind?

Oh, I don't know, Antonia hedges. It might be nice to get away. Chicago is a few weeks ahead of Vermont in spring weather. As if her whole reason for going to Tilly's is to check in on her sister's daffodils.

Well, whatever, I think it's a great idea, Izzy opines. Antonia is always impressed by other people's certainties—she often has to borrow from their assurances to make up her own mind. Along with their checkbook, decision-making was another area of their lives she ceded to Sam. He never second-guessed himself, never fished any of his cast-off bread back out of the waters. A good cop with no self-doubt. Was that a good thing for a cop? One of these days, she had cautioned herself, Sam would leave her, tired of her questions, of her intense need to get not just the words but the world right.

One of these days is here. Sam has left her, but not in the way she had feared.

Don't be so sure he isn't getting something out of it, her therapist had said, shaking her head, full of her own certainties. Have you ever asked yourself why he married you? Here's a thought, the therapist had offered, as if setting a piece of merchandise down on the counter for Antonia to consider buying. Maybe you are the one carrying the doubts in the relationship? Maybe your husband needs the balance of a highly sensitive wife? Maybe Sam isn't all that sure himself where Burkina Faso lies?

THREE

Rules of the sisterhood

Her sister is waiting at baggage claim. Antoni-AH! Tilly shouts, making a point of calling Antonia by the name she prefers, rather than by Toni, the childhood nickname the extended family still insists on using.

People turn to look. Foreigners with loud voices, expressive faces, gesticulating. Pipe down, their American classmates were always hushing them those first years after their arrival.

The two sisters hug, let go, hug again, ready, not ready to let go.

The first rule of sisterhood: *Always act pleased to see them.*

Antonia *is* pleased to see Tilly. They are the middle sisters—Izzy and Mona at either end. A mere eleven months separate each sister from the next in line. Sometimes it feels as if only together are they a whole person—referred to reverentially as "the sisterhood."

Antonia and Tilly last saw each other in Vermont right after Sam's death. Tilly flew in the morning after. The first responder of all Antonia's friends and family.

But then, that's always been Tilly's role. She is the doer—whether true or not anymore, by now their roles have self-perpetuating lives of their own. The mask stuck to the face; take it off at your own peril. Who am I going to be anymore? Antonia had asked Tilly in the wake of the wake. No longer a teacher at the college, no longer volunteering and serving on a half dozen boards, no longer in the thick of the writing whirl—she has withdrawn from every narrative, including the ones she makes up for sale. Who am I? the plaintive cry.

I don't know. Tilly had shrugged, eyebrows and shoulders riding up, emphasizing the extent of her ignorance. Ask your sisters, Tilly had advised. I'm no good at all that shrink stuff.

Apparently, they've divvied up the skills in the sisterhood. You need something done, funeral meats and cheeses set out on the table after a memorial service—that's where Tilly shines. In emotional anguish—you aren't sure what you want, whether to leave or not leave your philandering husband, throw in the towel on a friendship, call Izzy. For answers of the miscellaneous kind—the perfect breed of dog, the real estate market, the best shampoo for thinning hair, Mona's your gal.

So, what can Antonia contribute to the sisterhood? Its pundit, with a head full of quotes? Its nervous system, as a highly sensitive person? But all the sisters are nervous types, high strung.

Whoever she will be now, she knows better than to trespass into another sister's domain. *Honor thy sister's turf*, another of the rules of the sisterhood.

WELCOME TO ILL-Y-NOISE, Tilly jokes, imitating their father. Ill-y-noise, Papi would parse out the name. How can it be a good place to live with a name like that? Now that he's gone, his corny jokes are part of their nostalgia riffs. Papi was always trying to convince Tilly to move east with the grandchildren, closer to Mami and him. Of course, bring Kaspar, too, Papi added if prodded—the sons-in-law always an afterthought with paterfamilias.

Where's Kaspar? Antonia asks out of politeness. When Tilly first introduced her husband-to-be to the sisterhood, they didn't think he'd be a keeper. He took himself too seriously. He might be a math-whiz scientist, but his sense of humor was in the minus numbers.

So are you a friendly ghost? Izzy had jokingly asked him.

I beg your pardon, he had replied.

But Kaspar has stuck around almost forty years.

Is he double parked? Antonia asks now, feigning concern.

Hell, no, Tilly laughs, her smoker's cough exploding, giving heft to her laughter. I drove. Will wonders never cease? Tilly, who never drives on highways because, she says, highways have too many cars. That's like saying a city has too many people, Antonia likes to tease her. Fuck you! Tilly's response to any mockery is to cuss loudly—no matter where she is. Zero self-control.

By the way, Mona tells me you didn't believe me that my daffodils were up, Tilly reports. So you think it's all a pigment of my imagination?

Figment, Antonia corrects. Figment of your imagination.

Up yours. Tilly curls her upper lip.

So what else did Mona tell you? Antonia probes. Though she hates these sisterhood triangulations, bifurcations, she can't help wanting to know the current Sturm und Drang. They might be one whole person, but not without constant altercations, meltdowns, hurt feelings. It's exhausting.

As she drives, Tilly rummages in her purse for a piece of gum to mask her smoker's breath so that Kaspar doesn't smell it. She adjusts the bobbing dog with a neck spring attached to the dashboard to help her spot her car in parking lots. The doer cannot not do. But it means she misses her exit, and they have to drive ten miles out of the way. Just as well. Tilly knows a coffee shop where they can sit and gossip. The place also has an outdoor patio where Tilly can smoke.

It's too cold, Antonia says, shaking her head.

No, it's not. They argue about whether it's too cold or not. This time, though, Tilly acquiesces. It's Antonia's birthday tomorrow, first one without Sam. You deserve to be spoiled.

Deserve, mi-sherve, Antonia scoffs. The verb annoys her—the whole idea that you are entitled to special treatment, a sense of grievance when life doles out to you what it doles out to everybody: mortality, sorrow, loss.

Don't knock it, sister. Nice to be spoiled. So anyhow, what made you change your mind and come?

What do you mean *what*? To see you, of course. She doesn't want to get into the mixed bag of her motivations.

They sit quietly for a moment, holding hands, a rare

quiet respite in their hectic sistering. All those moments she was too busy to help Sam dig up his potatoes in the garden, to come quick to the window and see an unusual bird that just landed on the feeder. There will be a lot of these little kicks at her heart in the days, months, years to come.

THEY BUS THEIR own table, still Mami's daughters long after there is a mother to be daughters of. So, what are you up for? Tilly asks. Want to go to the Vietnamese market? There's also treasure-hunting at secondhand shops. A neat little bistro on the way home, where they can have a glass of wine, rum, vodka. Along with being a smoker, Tilly is the serious drinker of the four. Anything special Antonia wants? Just say the word.

She wants Sam is what Antonia wants, but that is not one of the offerings. How about I shadow you through a typical day.

I don't get it, Tilly says, frowning.

Act like I'm not here, Antonia elaborates.

Why would I want you to visit and then pretend you're not here?

I get to have a little window on your life. Then, when I'm in Vermont, I can imagine what you are doing at any given moment.

Tilly's frown deepens. I'm not *that* predictable. Do you know at any given time what you'll be doing?

Of course, Antonia does. Even if she were not grieving, she knows that at six every morning, she'll be doing her yoga exercises while listening to her bird CDs, the singsong of the robin, the three-or-more repetitions of the mockingbird, the whiney notes of the goldfinch. It would actually be a comfort knowing that at that exact moment Tilly is drinking her coffee, listening to the news while prepping for the meals ahead, running a load of laundry—Tilly is a multitasker, a doer on steroids. Whenever Antonia calls, she can hear pots banging, a hose spraying, Tilly peeing, Tilly taping up the package she will have already mailed to Vermont for Antonia's birthday, thinking that Antonia won't be coming to Chicago to shadow her as she goes about her day.

I still don't get it, Tilly says after listening to Antonia's explanation. But then, you always had to be different from us.

So, will that continue to be her role going forward? The one who defines herself by being what the others are not?

THEY MAKE THE rounds of a typical Tilly day. At the Vietnamese market, Tilly fills up her cart with items Antonia recognizes from Tilly's periodic care packages:

dried mushrooms, candied ginger, boxes of teas with Chinese characters, peeled garlic in a jar. The store is pungent with nostalgic smells, reminding Antonia of mercados back home in the DR, she and her sisters trailing behind Mami and the tías down rows of piled vegetables, fruits fly-speckled, bloody strips of meat hanging from hooks, a calf bawling in the abattoir next door. Such are the madeleines that recall the sisterhood's island childhood.

But Tilly's favorite activity is shopping in the second-hand shops that abound in her suburb. They all have playful names, as if poking fun at their own con, selling people's discards: Sweet Charity, Déjà New, and the too-cute Twice Loved, which Tilly says used to be a sewing shop named Son of a Stitch that closed up. The owner got a lot of flak from what Tilly calls—with the same intonation with which she curses—Christians.

Tilly has often complained about her evangelical neighborhood. We have more churches per square root than anywhere, she says authoritatively, and Antonia doesn't have the heart to correct her speech or question her statistics. Leave it for Mona to challenge the numbers. Anyhow, Tilly says, one neighbor in particular, a gossip and troublemaker, brought over an Easter basket when Tilly's kids were little. Along with dyed eggs and jelly beans there was a little bottle of red dye and four nails. I mean, give me a break! Tilly shakes her head. Ruining a three- and five-year-old's Easter by bringing up the crucifixion!

Well, that is what Easter is, Antonia could have defended the woman. She has heard Tilly's story before, but she listens again without commentary. It gives Tilly such pleasure to tell it. Part of Antonia's turf, storytelling, which she periodically relinquishes to the others. Give them a turn to tell the story.

So I told her we were Jewish. Ha! It was like I'd personally crucified Jesus myself. Soon thereafter, the neighbor moved away. Tilly gloats, exactly what she had hoped for. That bitch was like a wolf in cheap clothing!

Antonia laughs but, again, offers no correction. Tilly laughs too, thinking it's her story that has amused her sister.

In every shop, the salesladies—they are mostly women—are effusive about Tilly. We love your sister. It's nice to see that Tilly has made her mark here. She has always been the low-profile sister, letting the others win the prizes, get the As and the attention. Give her her cigarettes, a bottle of rum, someone to screw. You guys are the stars, she always would say to Izzy and Antonia growing up. What about me? baby sister Mona would pipe in, aggrieved.

You're the fucking meteor! Tilly would howl with laughter. She was the first to enjoy her own jokes.

In that book Antonia will probably never write on the lives of the anonymous, she'll advance her theory about people who are the salt of the earth, the laborers in the vineyard, the migrant workers, the unremarkable siblings. They do not need to be famous, important, visible; there is an aggression to fame, a violence to it, whereas anonymity is companionable; we're all in this together; first, I bring my girlfriend, then I help you bring yours. *I'm nobody! Who are you?* So many stray lines from her teaching days.

You are soooo lucky to have her as a sister, one saleslady gushes at their third stop. The older woman, petite and perky—sparkly earrings matching her sparkly eyes—has been following Antonia through the store, highlighting this sweater or that set of glasses they just got in. Your sister is so special, the saleslady keeps saying.

She's amazing, isn't she? I'm very lucky. Thanks for your help, Antonia says, hoping to conclude the chat. Unlike its positive effect on Tilly, all this friendliness is getting on her nerves.

Let's not go to any more stores, Antonia suggests when they exit the shop.

I thought you wanted to see what I do with my day?

How about what you do besides shop?

They drive over to the gym where Tilly is enrolled in several elder exercise classes. A quick tour of the place, she promises. The old Black man at the reception desks asks Tilly, Where's my hug? Everyone missed her today in class. I've met the nicest people here, Tilly claims. Nobody's perfect in an elder exercise class—everyone's fat, hurting from arthritis, needing to recover some skill they've lost. We love each other as we are, Tilly brags.

Some people would say that's a definition of Christianity, Antonia points out to get a rise from her sister.

Go to hell, Tilly curses.

On the way home from her typical day, Tilly brings up Izzy again. So, has Felicia been in touch?

Good thing she's not here to hear you, Antonia banters back. Izzy is particular about people not using her given name. She hates Felicia. What a setup! Like I'm supposed to always be happy or something. Truth is, except for Tilly, the other sisters are particular, too. Mona hates Ramona—used only by their mother in scolding mode—and Antonia doesn't like anyone using her nickname. Tilly, meanwhile, says call her whatever the fuck you want: Tilly, Matilda, fine with her.

Antonia recounts her recent conversation with Izzy. The cultural center, the Latino takeover of Western Mass. Yet one more of Izzy's grandiose ideas. Hopefully, it won't happen, and Izzy will settle down to the humble job of taking care of herself.

I guess you haven't heard the latest? Tilly interrupts. She's going to buy an abandoned motel.

A motel? What for?

To house the artists, of course, Tilly says, as if Antonia is a dummy to ask the obvious.

But she didn't mention a motel to me, and I just talked to her—what, two days ago?

It was right after the second Mario–Estela phone call. The thought of that reunion intrudes. Antonia wonders how it is going. Right before leaving, she bought the bus ticket online for Estela to pick up at the downtown bus station in Denver. Who will Mario get to give him a ride to Burlington to pick her up? Roger, or maybe the woman they call when all else fails? Mama Terry, the nickname the migrant community has given the gray-haired, Spanish-speaking gringa, who will procure whatever service you need: from rides to airports, grocery stores, doctors' offices to female company, Vermont girls strapped for cash who want to make extra money on the side or girls in need of company themselves.

I guess a lot can happen overnight with Izzy, Antonia concedes. But where's she getting the money to fund this grand plan?

I think her house finally sold or is selling. She might still have some money from what we inherited. Or maybe she won the lottery. She's always buying tickets. You never know with Izzy. Tilly is shaking her head. The truth is they really need to do something about their big sister. Remember at the memorial?

Izzy hadn't appeared, so they started the service without her. When she finally did arrive, she couldn't sit still, roaming around the church, taking pictures on her cell phone, a closeup of the candles burning, of the flowers, of the minister at the lectern. Mona had to escort Izzy back to their pew, but Izzy broke loose, climbed up to the choir loft in the back of the church to take photos of the tops of everybody's head. *What Sam sees now*, she captioned the photo she texted to her sisters, and then just as the minister was concluding, *We all go down to the dust but even at the grave we make our song, alleluia, alleluia*—almost as if Izzy had timed it, with that uncanny aptness of the crazed—pings went off on her sisters' phones in the congregation.

Tilly and Antonia laugh. This is serious, they keep reminding each other, which makes them laugh all the harder, edging closer to the line where hilarity turns into tears.

I've actually been thinking of coming east. Tilly lays out a plan she has been hatching with Mona: she flies into Boston, Mona flies up from North Carolina, and Antonia drives down from Vermont, then they all converge on Western Mass, or wherever their gypsy sister will have landed for the moment. Get Izzy into some treatment center or other. A combined sisterhood reunion and rescue. What do you think?

That could work, Antonia says, a lukewarm response that amounts to a *no* in sisterhoodspeak. (*Never say an outright no to a sister*. Could be a rule, if it isn't already so.) But Antonia has no stomach for three sisters ganging up on the fourth. Not to mention that one at a time is her preferred mode of sisterhooding. Tilly by herself or Izzy or Mona, but all together, it's more than Antonia can handle, especially right now. Her highly sensitive personhood is already in overdrive.

Anyhow, it's an offer, take it or leave it. Frankly, Tilly adds—a speech mannerism she has picked up from Kaspar, like the pronouncement *the truth is*, which comes from their mother—frankly, and maybe she shouldn't say this, Tilly says, she is more worried about their big sister than she is about Antonia in her widowhood.

You always land on your feet, Tilly says.

Is that the truth? Antonia teases her sister, using her mother's voice.

Tilly takes a hand off the wheel to slap Antonia's arm. You bitch! Coming from any other sister, such foulmouthed name-calling would bring on a fight, ill feelings, the unloading of grievances going all the way back to childhood. But Tilly can get away with it. It's her form of affection, like the *-itos* at the ends of words in Spanish, making the world manageable, kid-size. Izzy always says it's what she most misses in English.

TILLY'S SMALL HOUSE on Happy Valley Road is busy with lawn ornaments, great deals from the resale shops: birdfeeders, houses, and baths; windchimes tinkling from a number of boughs. It looks tacky, an adjective Antonia does not like to associate with her kin, just as she would not want any of her sisters to espouse right-wing politics.

Before they can stop for Antonia to pretend to admire the clutter, the front door opens. Kaspar has been waiting for them. There's a rambling message from Izzy—he heard the phone, but he was on the toilet. They play back the voicemail: Izzy talking excitedly. She's in Western Mass. Soon as she takes care of some business, she's pulling an all-nighter and driving to Ill-y-noise. Izzy's voice cracks. Ay, Papi, I miss him so much. Anyhow, she concludes, I'm hoping to arrive in time to celebrate Antonia's birthday. It's a surprise. Don't tell her, okay?

Tilly and Antonia look at each other and burst out laughing. Your sister, Tilly says, shaking her head. It's how they refer to the outlier sister of the moment, as if she's for another sister to claim. Recently, it's almost always Izzy.

Tilly sighs, shaking her head. So much for their two-sister one-on-one. But what can they do if a sister invites herself along, as often happens when two meet up, the increased magnetic force drawing the others?

Why not just go ahead and ask Mona to come, too? Tilly proposes. They need to be together and rescue Izzy, get her back on track. Sixty-six and living like a burnt-out hippie in other people's houses. And now that she might have sold her own, she'll be even more rootless. She needs grounding, a home, a companion, medication.

Tilly and Antonia try calling Mona to suggest the plan— but their sister is not available to take their call. It's urgent, Tilly leaves a message. Surely Mona will agree to join them, as she's the one who has been pushing for an intervention for months. Plus, baby sister does not like being left out.

The small house on Happy Valley Road hums with activity. Tilly and Antonia are a good team, the two middle-sister workhorses, making the spare beds, setting out towels, vacuuming the carpets, interspersing these chores with calls to Izzy, whose phone instantly goes to voicemail, and to Mona—Tilly's messages increasingly pissy. Kaspar is commissioned to drive over to Caputo's, where there's a good wine selection, a large assortment of cheeses, fresh pastas; he's to take his cell phone along just in case they think of something else they need but have forgotten in their haste.

When Mona finally returns their call, Tilly outlines the plan.

Sorry, Charlie, Mona says. Too last-minute; I can't just drop everything. Even though she is winding down her practice, she still has some clients. I have a life.

We all do, Tilly rebuts. Bickering ensues. Who has a life, who doesn't.

Bitch! Tilly finally shouts, and hangs up.

Come on, be fair, Antonia counsels. We sprung it on her. Call her back.

You call her back! Tell her it's what you want for your birthday.

By now, Antonia is too caught in the strong current of sisterhood to know what she wants. She hits redial on Tilly's cell. The phone rings once. Bitch, yourself! Mona screams in her ear.

It's me, Antonia corrects the understandable mistake. Mona bursts out crying. Tilly hung up on her. She's so unfair. I know, Mo-mo, Antonia soothes the baby sister. It's just we're worried and we need you, we miss you, we love you. You catch more flies with sugar than you do with salt, Mami would say. Please come. It's what I want for my birthday.

Mona grumpily agrees, but with a caveat: she'll come only if Tilly apologizes first. Another standoff. By the time Antonia has convinced Tilly to go the extra mile— it's what she wants from Tilly for her birthday—a call comes in from Izzy: she'll be arriving later than she thought, as she is now pulling a trailer behind her.

A trailer? Tilly is alarmed. Did you buy a motel *and* a mobile home?

Whatever Izzy's response, it's at such a volume that Tilly has to hold the phone away from her ear. She curses, but not loudly and not into the mouthpiece.

Ask her where she is, Antonia mouths.

But Izzy has already hung up. When they try calling her back, the number she called from is not her number. Hi, this is Phil. Leave me a message.

Who the hell is Phil? Tilly records her message: Hey, Phil!—like she knows who he is. We're calling my sister Izzy. Can you tell her to please call me back?

You're not going to believe this, Tilly says to Kaspar, as he comes in the door with the commissioned purchases. First, she needs a drink. They clink glasses, standing in the kitchen, shaking their heads in commiseration. Kaspar questions the sisters as if they can divine Izzy's motives or make sense of her choices. Who would be crazy enough to drive a trailer in March with the weather so unpredictable? Is she moving in or what?

Tilly and Antonia exchange a look. The truth is, it's a good thing we're doing this interjection now, Tilly says.

Intervention, Antonia corrects.

Screw you! Tilly glowers, pouring herself another drink. Kaspar purses his lips in disapproval. There's no call for that, he chides his wife.

Tilly turns away and gives Kaspar a middle finger for only Antonia to see. It's like Tilly never left high school, Antonia thinks. Just as Izzy never left childhood, and baby Mona never left the womb. And she? What stage in life would her sisters say Antonia is stuck in?

THAT NIGHT, TILLY crawls in bed with Antonia. She uses the remote to turn on the news; both sisters are too agitated to sleep. It's a habit Antonia has become well-acquainted with in her empty house, turning on the news—in her case the radio—for company, her own sadness put in perspective by the larger sadness of the world.

The screen explodes with the sounds and sights of urgency. A swarm of police cars, wailing ambulances; lights panning the street; people shouting, screaming, calling for help; a breathless reporter is speaking earnestly into a microphone. Another mass shooting, this time in New Zealand.

The horror! the horror! enters the house on Happy Valley Road, making its way into the bedroom on its small, furred feet. The world is crazy. And their sister Izzy has lost her way in it, and they, the sisters, must intervene, get her back on track.

At least she's not in New Zealand, Tilly tries lamely for humor.

Please turn that off, Antonia pleads.

Tilly acquiesces but not without a jab at Antonia. You always have to get your way.

They lie in the dark, trading stories of the past, trying to track down when it was that they first noted big sister going off the rails.

Remember those fits she used to throw as a little kid? Hitting her head on the floor if you thwarted her? How she used to pull out her hair and had this huge bald spot? Or the time she tried to get a hold of Michelle Obama to offer to design her inauguration gown? Never mind that Izzy couldn't even sew a button on a blouse. How she fell in love with the worst men and turned away the sweet ones. I like a challenge, she'd say. Like she wasn't enough of a challenge to herself. Outrageous, hilarious, over the top—they've always laughed at Izzy's antics—but in a certain light, weren't these signs of a disconnect with reality that, untreated, has now become dangerous to Izzy herself? Antonia talks on and on before she realizes Tilly is snoring.

It's not like we ever had a choice, Tilly says from inside her dream, apropos of nothing Antonia can figure out.

ANTONIA'S BIRTHDAY DAWNS gray and worrisome. Outside, there's a chill wind blowing, the chimes are clanging, a jarring sound that goes right through her. They are tolling for Christchurch, Sam, Estela, Mario, Izzy. Not sci-fi, the ringtone du jour, but this clamoring of metal. The din of the inferno.

They haven't heard from Izzy again, though Antonia expects that, today being her birthday, Izzy will be calling. A date she's not likely to forget, as it marks the four-week overlap between their two birthdays, when they are the same age. It used to grate on Izzy when they were kids, to be reminded by Antonia: I'm as old as you are!

I'm as old as you are! You can't boss me around! Which is why Antonia's birthday would have to be engraved in Izzy's memory. Since as far back as Antonia can remember, Izzy has been the first to call and wake her up on her birthday singing "Las Mañanitas."

They keep trying her number, but their calls instantly go into voicemail. It might be out of charge, Kaspar suggests, a not unlikely possibility given how remiss Izzy is with practicalities.

So, do we call the police? Tilly asks, curling her upper lip with distaste. The sisters all have an aversion to authority, an immigrant thing, they think, compounded by their hippie pasts.

But what do they report? Felicia Isabel Vega is missing? But they can't be sure. Knowing Izzy, she might have found someone on the side of the road who needed a ride several states over. She might have discovered an alternative location for her Latino center and checked herself into a roadside motel, waiting till morning to call local real estate agents about possible properties for sale.

They wait, all morning, most of the afternoon. Soon, it's time to go pick up Mona at the airport. Kaspar comes along and waits outside in the car while the two sisters run in, glad for the distraction of orchestrating their reunion with Mona, texting back and forth, minutely tracking where she is, as if remotely landing a capsule from outer space. As they wait, Tilly looks around warily. New Zealand is on their minds. To tell you the truth, I feel weird anymore in airports, she says. I mean, doesn't that man over there look suspicious?

What man? Antonia asks. Either everyone looks suspicious or no one does.

Tilly points.

Oh my God, Tilly! Antonia pulls her sister's hand down. She is having a hard enough time managing one sister, how will she manage with two or possibly three sisters: one on a manic high, another with no self-control, a third arriving with grievances to sort? Remember, be nice, Antonia reminds Tilly when they spot Mona coming down the escalator, already looking irritated. It's what I want for my birthday.

Tilly emits a low snarl, an animal in attack mode. But she drops her attitude to wave eagerly at Mona. And, Antonia notes, Tilly does not call out Bitch! for hello. The sister does have some self-control, after all.

MONA AND TILLY gossip on the drive to Happy Valley Road. Tilly has scaled back on her catering. Mona is shifting her therapy practice to just dogs. No, no, no. Not a therapist *for* dogs, but a therapist using dogs with trauma victims. The kids are fine, Tilly recounts. A big contract.

A new house. A hard time juggling motherhood with a full-time job. Promotions, demotions, the stock market of life. The grandkids are incredible, beautiful, bright, destined for glory, as all grandkids are. (Antonia wouldn't dare say so, but it does seem all her friends who are grandparents and in every other way modest boast unabashedly about their extraordinary grandchildren. Who is having the unremarkable babies anymore? she'd ask Sam after a dinner party in which cell phone videos of little Sophie or Olivia or Timothy made the rounds at the table.) Their only flaw is they do not speak Spanish. What a shame. Or German, Kaspar puts in from the front seat. Monolinguals, he mutters, as if it were a vitamin deficiency that will come back later to haunt them.

The three sisters are in back, Kaspar alone in front, relegated to chauffeur, the gofers all the brothers-in-law become when the sisters are together. Antonia would just as soon have sat quietly in the front with Kaspar. But even though she is not saying much of anything, her presence is required.

In the past few years, even before Sam's death, Antonia has often felt disconnected from her sisters. (*Don't ever let on that you can survive, or would want to, without them.*) She has snapped off the thread that strung them together. Maybe it was the influence of Sam's equanimity and his quieter, consistent affections. Her own family felt so reactive, hyper, over the top—not just Izzy. Papi with his disownings. Mami's meltdowns. The shouting, the threats, the beatings with a belt, followed by profuse apologies and gifts.

What's a matter, birthday girl? her sisters keep asking Antonia, and then Mona answers for her. It's so unfair that this is happening on your birthday.

Antonia shrugs. But in the dark of the car, the shrug goes unnoticed. It's not like the Fates would call a moratorium on wickedness: Wait! Wait! Let's not ruin Antonia's day. Let's have the Christchurch shooting the day after her birthday.

You're being so quiet, Mona keeps prodding. Is something wrong?

Just listening, Antonia says. And then, to make her point, she asks if she has ever told them about what the quiet man says at a dinner party in one of Kingsolver's novels?

Before she can go on with the story, Tilly and Mona cut her short with a peal of laughter. Yes, sister, we have heard that quote many, many times. Her tediousness is reassuring. They go back to their gossip, as Antonia looks out the window, her reflection superimposed on the endless strip of shops, malls, gas stations flashing by, all vulnerable to someone with a gun in their backpack, an explosive device strapped to their belly, someone intent on doing harm.

She shakes away the horror. A nibble, a sip, the narrow path.

It's that time of day when the waning light can put her in a dark mood. She thinks of Demeter punishing the earth for the disappearance of her daughter. One loss Antonia doesn't have to anticipate or experience, as she has never had a daughter. No hay mal que por bien no venga, Mami would say. But then, Antonia will never experience the ground-shifting love of a mother for her daughter. She has had twinges of what that might feel like, over the years, with Tilly's kids, her friends' kids, a few special students. And most recently with Mario and Estela, pangs she has told herself she cannot afford to indulge now.

Shall we take a vote? Tilly is asking. Antonia has lost track of what it is they're voting on. Whether to head for the police station or not. Her two sisters concur, Kaspar disagrees, and Antonia, the tie-breaker, betrays the sisterhood by casting her vote with the brother-in-law. They should all take a step back, make some other calls—Izzy's old friends back in Boston; wasn't there a recent love interest?; their last remaining aunt, whom Izzy sometimes listens to—before they react.

It's a gloomy night, but they soldier on, Antonia's

birthday supper, after all. Tilly has prepared a special
meal of Antonia's favorite foods Antonia doesn't recall
being favorites, but she obliges. By now she has become
that fictive being, the sisterhood Antonia, with tastes
and predilections attached to her. She plays the part,
exclaiming over the stuffed peppers, roasted squash
with gruyere, spinach soufflé—the platters keep coming
to the table. Did Tilly invite a whole village to Antonia's
sixty-sixth birthday party?

Tilly clears the dinner plates, insisting everyone stay
put, and after much clattering, and a quiet hiatus in
which the side door creaks open—Tilly stepping out for
a smoke, no doubt—she returns, bearing a wedding-size
cake, blazing with what must be two dozen candles.
Feliz cumpleaños, she sings, and Mona and Kaspar join
in. Make a wish! they all insist. Antonia closes her eyes,
her first birthday without Sam, Izzy missing, the shooting in Christchurch, the dark mood ambushes her again.
She lets out the sob she cannot contain, tears streaming
down her cheeks. Mona and Tilly swoop to her side,
alarmed. ¿Qué te pasa? ¿Qué te pasa? All it takes is one
sister, and soon, they are all bawling.

Never remain dry-eyed when a sister is crying:
another rule of the sisterhood.

FOUR

To be missing is not a crime

I t is not a crime to go missing, Officer Morgan informs them. If you are an adult you can disappear, and it's your own darn business. However, in one of those conundrums of law enforcement, such persons should be reported promptly. For although nothing can be done, strictly speaking, the authorities want to know if someone has exercised their freedom as an adult to go missing.

The sisters express their surprise. They were convinced that the police would jump all over this case. What about all those shows on TV?

That's not the way it works, Officer Morgan clues

them in on the intricacies of the law. He has an unkempt look about him, overweight, pale, with tiny nicks on his jaw.

Mona, whom their mother often said should have been a lawyer, points out that this is totally ridiculous, a catch-22 situation. Officer Morgan frowns; he doesn't understand what Mona is referring to. Antonia flashes baby sister a cautionary look: *Romona, por favor. We need the cops on our side.*

It's a novel, Antonia clarifies. How easily she slips into her former teacher role. Have you ever read it?

No, ma'am, he has not. When would he have time to read with three kids to take care of? (Divorced, widowed? He doesn't say.) Always on the go, which might be why he has nicked himself shaving. His face looks like it got scratched up by one of the suspects his fellow officers brought in, before they were able to wrestle the offender to the ground.

The sisters have driven over to the station to file a report, leaving Kaspar behind to man the landline. They couldn't bear waiting one minute longer; even Antonia changed her nay vote. Kaspar tried to calm them. Let's be reasonable. There's probably a good explanation. We can call the police tomorrow. No need to drive over there tonight.

The guy seriously doesn't get it, Mona muttered. It's like his heart's in his head.

Remember he's not Dominican, Tilly defended Kaspar. He's really a good husband. He's never left me, Tilly elaborated when asked for good-husband specifics. He's not violent. He likes my cooking.

The description left Antonia feeling sad. The great loves they had all dreamed about as young women, reduced to the dubious compliment of horrors averted: at least I didn't marry an ax murderer, at least he's not a criminal, at least he didn't kill his father and marry his mother. That way lies literature.

We're the ones with strong emotions, the ones with heart, Mona asserted. Okay to give themselves all the attractive adjectives, the ethnic profiling they deplore admissible if one is a member of a targeted population.

Officer Morgan keeps referring to Felicia Vega. (*She'll kill you if she hears you call her that!* As with many of her thoughts, Antonia keeps this one to herself. Not a good idea to threaten a police officer—even if only by way of a figure of speech.) She actually goes by Izzy, Antonia finally corrects him. As for Izzy's profession, she used to work as a therapist in a group practice. She retired a couple of years ago.

A photo would be helpful, Officer Morgan says.

Incredibly, the sisters discover none of them has a photo of Izzy on her cell phone. It's like they're making her up. We'll email you one from home, Tilly promises.

How about her vitals? Any identifying marks? Piercings, tattoos, scars?

The sisters close their eyes, each one doing her own memory scan of Izzy's body. There's some debate about her height: five foot three or four, no way she's five foot five, as she likes to give out; weight, anywhere from a hundred to a hundred and fifteen pounds, up and down depending on her moods and diets. Remember her breatharian phase? Mona reminds her sisters. Izzy was convinced she could survive on air and sunlight? The sisters launch into storytelling. Officer Morgan keeps running his hand over his face like it's a magic slate he can wipe clean. The chip on her upper front tooth from when she fell on her face as a kid showing off she could fly from a not-too-high branch of a backyard tree; her really skinny, narrow feet, making it hard to find shoes that fit; her nails bitten down to the quick, and oh!—

She has this tiny birthmark on her left wrist in the shape of a plane, Antonia offers. Every time Izzy boarded a flight, she'd show off her birthmark. A santera, that's like a fortune-teller, predicted I would die in a plane crash, she'd announce to her seatmates, knowing full well what she was doing, drama queen that she was, always stirring things up. Not a good idea after 9-11 and the widespread fear of terrorists blowing up planes. A couple of times flight attendants had to ask her to keep her fortunes to herself or she'd have to be escorted off the flight.

Officer Morgan wipes his face again. They keep this up and he's going to tear that form up, Antonia reminds her sisters in Spanish.

When he's done being the amanuensis to all their stories, Officer Morgan begins tidying up his desk— signaling the conclusion of their interview, not unlike the custom back home of standing a broom by the door to let la visita know it's time for them to leave. He has done all he can do. He'll enter Felicia's information into his computer, but unless there is some proof of foul play or mental issues—and that, too, would need proof, he adds when their faces brighten—there's not much else he can do. There are several internet registries that the sisters can access on their own and post photos as well as all the statistics of the missing person, thereby broadcasting their search worldwide.

The officer takes down Tilly's home and cell numbers, Antonia and Mona's cell numbers, dismissing them finally with a noncommittal We'll keep an eye out.

These missing-person situations resolve themselves on their own 95 percent of the time.

Has the data behind this claim actually been gathered? Mona challenges. Another hand wipe across his face. A gesture he has repeated so many times, several nicks have started bleeding again, leaving tiny red teardrops like birthmarks all over the tired face.

WHAT A JERK! Mona vents in the car. Did you see how his whole face was full of scratches? I bet he beats his wife. I bet she tried to defend herself with her nails.

That's hilarious, Tilly says, riding Mona's riff. I bet that's why he was so la-di-da about Felicia Vega. She mimics his mispronunciation.

I can't believe he's never heard of Catch-22, Mona adds, one more demerit. I mean, it's even been on Jeopardy!

Her sisters are doing what they always do when they depart a scene, parsing the meat off its bones, analyzing, judging, exclaiming over the different personalities, a kind of sisterhood digestive system.

Come on, you guys, be fair, Antonia reminds them from the back seat.

How can you say that? He was a total idiot! Mona has turned around to face Antonia. The interior of the car is too dark for Antonia to see Mona's outraged expression, but she knows it's there.

BACK AT THE HOUSE, the three sisters commandeer Kaspar's laptop and spend the hours until dawn visiting all the missing-persons entries from Massachusetts to Illinois. Several times they have had to consult Google to figure out which states neighbor each other on the way to Tilly's. The only geography they were taught as children was of their half island.

Do they post a profile? Or would that bring on el fukú of bad luck? Maybe Kaspar is right? Maybe they're doing the familial overreaction and they just need to calm down? Officer Morgan said most times, especially with adults, these "disappearances" work themselves out. And Izzy loves the shock value of turning up when you least expect her.

As they scroll down the profiles of the missing, Antonia catches herself lingering among the entries. Maybe she'll spot a familiar face, Samuel Sawyer, 71, last seen on the way to his favorite restaurant one evening in late June to celebrate his wife's retirement.

MONA IS THE first to break down. She blames herself for not insisting earlier on an intervention. She has long suspected that Izzy was not well, and it's only gotten worse in the last couple of years. Izzy with her grandiose plans of saving the world, wildly ecstatic during her manic phases, then plunging into dark moods during which, like astronauts behind the moon, she cannot be reached. But they've gotten used to it, inured to Izzy's chronic craziness, even at times amused at how outrageous she can be. Bottom line, they've not wanted to be their sister's keeper. Living your own life is a full-time job. Mona bewails the fact that she doesn't even have a single photo of her sister on her iPhone, but dozens of shots of her dogs.

Your dogs are important, her sisters keep reminding her. Come on, Mo-mo. You can't blame yourself. It's nobody's fault.

Or everybody's fault, Antonia thinks, remembering the times she counseled Izzy to take care of herself so as not to become a burden on anyone else, code for *I'm overwhelmed by your needs*.

But Mona won't be comforted. She's on a roll, bending over, swaying and wailing, grieving in a way that feels ancient. She wants to know where her sister is! Izzy, who hasn't been in touch for now going on forty-eight hours, not even texting happy birthday to her momentary twin sister; Izzy, who called from somewhere in Western Mass, on her way to Ill-y-noise, after she took care of some business having to do with buying an abandoned motel to house her migrant artist revolution.

How crazy it all sounds. Antonia runs her hand over her face, recalling Officer Morgan's gesture. Three kids. How can he manage if he is divorced or widowed? Especially when he's on the night shift? Antonia's heart is momentarily heavy with his load.

The narrow path, the narrow path, she keeps pulling herself back. His burden is his, Mario's and Estela's theirs, and hers is hers. But Antonia is having trouble keeping everybody separate. *O, that way madness lies; let me shun that*, she reminds herself. It has always worked, a guardrail of the best that has been thought and said. *Culture is a great help out of our present difficulties*; she recalls a discussion over Matthew Arnold's essay. Her senior seminar looked doubtful. Kids raised on medications for attention deficits, anxiety, mood and behavior disorders. Meanwhile Antonia has read her Arnold; taken daily doses of her favorite poems, novels, plays; practiced meditation on and off for years.

But even so, she can't seem to ward off the dragons of the world. An ongoing problem, which is why she tends to be reclusive, constructing the firewall that others must have inbuilt as part of their healthy emotional operating system. She thinks of Officer Morgan on his night shift, calling home to check up on the kids, making sure they're not doing something they shouldn't be doing: visiting forbidden websites or watching naughty videos; reminding the oldest to heat up the macaroni and cheese in the fridge, feed his younger sibs, do the dishes. Good night then, say your prayers, Antonia imagines him saying. Be sure to lock the front and back doors, there are a lot of crazies out there—three of them have just visited the station, a fourth one is still on the loose.

THE SISTERS FINALLY decide to post a profile. Arguing the whole while about how to describe Izzy, even what picture to post, each one invoking what Izzy would want them to say, as if she is the target audience of the sketch they have titled "Beloved Sister." She already sounds like she's fucking dead, Tilly says, bawling.

The sisters check in with Officer Morgan or one of his colleagues several times a day. They've downloaded the Missing Person Checklist from outpostforhope.org. Made all the recommended phone calls, and then some: to family members, friends, former workplace, though Izzy hasn't been employed for the past couple of years. It turns out she was fired from the Spanish-language mental health practice she helped start. Something about Izzy not keeping sufficiently clear professional boundaries—at one point even hosting an ad hoc refugee camp in her basement, bereft abuelitas mourning their disappeared children and grandchildren. Izzy did get some sort of severance/disability package, and while they were still alive, a monthly allowance from their parents. She also recently sold her house, so there's that little stockpile, which is what she must be using to buy abandoned properties in Western Mass. Back in Boston, where she has been living, she seems to have been camping out with one friend or another, but then falling out with them and moving on. Only one friend, Maritza, recently heard from her. Izzy asked her to join the board of the Migrant Centro de Arte. I didn't have the heart to say no, Maritza explains.

Her sisters were asked as well, and none of them had the heart to say yes. Why encourage Izzy's craziness? But in spite of what the others have diagnosed as pathology, Antonia sometimes feels there is something noble about Izzy's "craziness." So unlike the ignoble craftiness and cunning she herself sometimes resorts to, part of the immigrant survival tool kit.

Maritza recalls the name of the town where the arts center is to be located. It sounds like *asshole*, Maritza says, spelling out the name, A-t-h-o-l. They Google the town, and there it is, in Worcester county.

The truth is, Tilly says, wagging her head.

What is the truth? Antonia jokes back.

You athol! Tilly grins, naughtily.

Even with Troy burning, the sisterhood can't help throwing fuel into the fire.

They call hospitals, highway police, homeless shelters, roadside motels along the Google-mapped routes from Athol to Happy Valley Road in Ill-y-noise. It's unreal, Antonia thinks, just the allegorical-sounding names are making her feel they've entered a modern-day *Pilgrim's Progress*. But what good is a Google map? Knowing their sister, there's no guarantee that Izzy would take either the fastest route or the scenic route or anything as straightforward as a route. Needle in a haystack doesn't begin to describe it. More like a single grain of sand on a windy beach of shifting dunes.

As the days go by, Antonia's homing instinct kicks in. She needs to get back, water her houseplants, fill her bird-feeders. Here at the very tail end of winter, the wrens, blue-birds, goldfinches are just beginning to arrive. This was supposed to be a short birthday trip, so she didn't even put a hold on her mail. The box must be full, a sure signal to burglars. Although, come to think of it, what's there to steal? The most valuable thing they could take is gone.

But it feels like a desertion to abandon the spot where Izzy was last headed, Tilly's house on the ironically named street in the aptly named state. And although Antonia is/was/evermore shall be known as the selfish sister who pulls away from the others, she is now—temporarily, she hopes—the oldest sister who has to take charge of the sisterhood, leave no stone unturned, until they've dug their big sister out from whichever one she has crawled under or, God forbid, been buried beneath.

A sip, a nibble, Antonia keeps reminding herself.

FINALLY, AFTER CLINGING to each other for over a week, and still no word from Izzy, the sisters come up with a plan. Mona will fly to Boston, lay over there for a few days, make a report at the local police department, talk to Maritza as well as Izzy's former neighbors, colleagues, old friends. Meanwhile, Tilly will drive the route their sister might have taken, put up posters at service stations and rest stops along the way. She has already taped one to her car, a shock to see Izzy's face blazoned on the side of Tilly's Toyota, as if their sister were running for office or advertising her arts center.

Since the sisters are dispersing, Antonia feels she can finally disentangle herself, go home and continue the online search from there for now. As Officer Morgan said, these disappearances usually resolve themselves. Izzy has to be *somewhere*! Same line of argument she has tried for Sam, with no positive results. The truth is, to quote Tilly and their mother, the truth is there is no truth she can rely on at all.

What else to do now before they part? Last on the Missing Person Checklist is: hire a private investigator. They interview several retired detectives whose names keep cropping up on the missing persons websites. None inspire confidence, though it could just be how Skype distorts faces, makes everyone look like they've been caught by a surveillance camera. The minimum charge is a hundred bucks an hour, about eight hundred a day, not including travel expenses, more for multiple state searches. Yikes! But this is no time to save for a rainy day. The downpour has come. Every day is critical, as Private Eye Kempowski reminds them. He wears a white shirt, a tie, gives off the vibes of an undertaker, Antonia can't help feeling. But Kempowski does have a 90 percent success rate for all missing persons he's been hired to find. Even Mona has lost her contentiousness and doesn't ask him to prove it.

To tell you the absolute truth, Kempowski says in a mournful tone—a phrase Antonia finds even more suspect than Tilly's telling truths—the absolute truth is that it's the 10 percent I haven't found who haunt me still.

It seems to Antonia that a haunted private eye who

deals in absolutes is not the best candidate to discover Izzy's whereabouts. But then, stranger things have been happening. The world is crazy. Mona is absolutely right.

ON HER WAY home from the airport in Burlington, Antonia's spirits plummet. The drive has beautiful views of the lake, the Green Mountains, the Adirondacks, rays of light filtering through breaks in the clouds, creating radiant spotlights, God highlighting some beloved patch in his creation. But who to turn to and say, Look at that? Better to note the sad, dreary things she wouldn't want to share with anyone. The trees have not yet leafed out, forlorn clumps of abandoned nests visible in their skeletal branches. The birds are few and far between—they probably know not to head north until they can be sure their birdfeeder stops are stocked. The lake looks glassy, reflecting a gray sky. But even that can be deceptive. The thin ice. Children skating on a pond at the edge of the woods. Maybe Antonia herself will go missing, drive south until the hills turn emerald and the sky a tender blue that triggers wonder wonder wonder.

Hello, Sam! she hollers inside the sealed car. Come on! Give me one little sign: a cloud in an arresting shape, a tiny plane with a thick, satisfying contrail, to let me know you're there. Any sign will do.

That way lies madness. Antonia pulls back from the edge, reminding herself to think of the positive. For one thing, it is a relief to get away from the hothouse of the sisterhood. But she also misses them, Tilly and Mona, and oh God, Izzy. Antonia has already texted them, including Izzy. *Landed Vermont. Missing you all.* Good thing about texting, simple, easily communicable, emoticon-friendly sentiments. No mixed feelings.

She takes the turn off the highway, winds her way to her dirt road, past houses whose residents she knows after thirty years: ancient Mrs. Gaudet, lost her own husband decades ago (nights, when Antonia's coming home late, she notes the forlorn little light at one window—kitchen, bedroom, bathroom?); the former French teacher and her live-in companion, their two Adirondack chairs like sunflowers in the summer, shifting across the lawn over the course of the day to face full sun; the rundown house with its flagpole and raggedy flag and a cranky lady in a cardigan who never says hi; the rental house whose shifting tenants always seem to have kids who leave their cheap plastic toys strewn on the dirt yard; the spiffed-up house the gay couple surrounded with a high hedge, probably to shield themselves from the sight of those plastic toys. Then, her next-door neighbor, Roger.

As she drives by the farm, Antonia wonders how

the Estela-Mario reunion has gone. On and off, she has thought of them. Did Estela catch the bus east? Who did Mario enlist to pick her up at the Burlington bus station? What is the living situation like? Has Roger relented? Antonia could turn into his place, park in front of the trailer, knock and ask, ¿Cómo están? But this would be to encourage an ongoing dependency, which, like Officer Morgan with his reading, Antonia just doesn't have the energy for right now.

Remember to take care of the caretaker, Outpost for Hope included on its downloadable checklist for families of missing persons. *You're entitled to a little TLC yourself.* Antonia is missing two of the people she most loved in the world. Still, she dislikes these back-patting encouragements, *entitled*, *deserve*. You need a little me-time, a former colleague had recommended to Antonia when they bumped into each other in town. It smacks of a privileged mindset that believes itself exempt from the ills the rest of the world has to contend with. Antonia recalls the reporter in front of a devastated neighborhood in post-Katrina New Orleans noting with astonishment: We're used to scenes like this in Haiti or Africa, but this isn't supposed to happen here. Antonia played the clip to her classes. Does suffering hurt less if you're poor? she asked the room full of young students.

Only the silent dark looks of her two minority students signaled to Professor Vega that they got what she
was talking about.

But even though she disapproves of the attitude,
Antonia finds herself partaking of that same privileged
prerogative. Why should so much be heaped on her? I'm
not Job, she reminds the God she only consults when
she is feeling overwrought. Shades of Mami. So many
promesas made and broken once it was clear God was
not going to cede control. Maybe the only difference
between Antonia and the blithe partakers is that she recognizes what she is doing.

And what good does that do anyone? She imagines
Sam dismissing her easy exonerations. And maybe that
is how he will keep coming back: periodically breaking through the firewalls of her narrow path with his
insights, suggestions, questions.

AND THERE IT IS, perched on top of the hill, the dream
house Sam built on a small subdivision of their former lot,
now left for her to inhabit alone, every detail something
he researched: the awning windows that never allow rain
to blow in; the doorknobs with levers instead of knobs,
easier for them to handle as they grew old; the slate from
a local quarry; the heated concrete floors; the CERV

unit—she has no idea how it works. What normally brought pleasure, the sight of it there, quickening her heart as she approached, now brings on that ache in her chest. She recalls friends consoling her after Sam's service, saying that the hole in her heart would heal with time. But Antonia suspects this is not quite what will happen. More likely she will learn to live with a hole in her heart.

She pulls into her driveway, hits the button for the garage door on *her* side, avoiding the sight of the empty space to the left of her car where Sam's pickup used to be parked, now given away to the Good News garage up in Burlington that refurbishes used cars to donate to the needy, something she knows Sam would approve of— again, how he lives on, in her choices and in the vehicle's afterlife. As she turns off the car, she notices the back door of the garage is ajar. In her avoidance of looking over to his side, she must have forgotten to lock it before she left home over a week ago. A burglar could have come in, walked across the space where Sam's pickup used to be, and entered the house through the mudroom. What a good laugh Sam would have, pointing out how all her caution and precaution have again come to naught.

You never know, she always remarked, while also envying him his role as the trusting guy, the good cop. It's not just the sisters with assigned roles. Maybe it's part and parcel of being connected to others whom you have to discriminate a self from.

Now she hears a rustling sound from Sam's side of the garage; an arrow of fear hits a bull's-eye in her heart. Here it is at last: the day that she predicted, a burglar in wait for her to come home, and Sam not alive for her to tell him I told you so. But more likely it's an animal, a raccoon or maybe a skunk, that got in somehow and couldn't get out. Antonia turns cautiously to gaze into the dark corner, the garage door already having descended behind her. A human shape emerges from a nest made of patio-furniture cushions stacked on the floor, a big birdseed bag for a pillow. A girl or maybe a woman, hard to tell. The eyes are luminous pockets in her brown face, the black hair with strands escaping from the long braid. She seems to have been napping, and Antonia's unexpected arrival has startled her awake.

Not a threatening burglar but a frightened girl, the smell of her now apparent, a body that hasn't bathed in days. She stands up ready to bolt, and that's when Antonia notices the large belly, so very pregnant that she might have come into the garage the way a wild animal seeks out a lair to give birth to its young.

¿Qué te pasa? Antonia asks, some trigger in her brain telling her to speak in Spanish. The girl has to be Estela.

And that's right. Antonia counts back. Roger gave her a week's reprieve, so this must mean her welcome next door ran out. And that belly couldn't have made things any easier with Roger. Sly young fox, Mario, not to mention his girlfriend was pregnant.

¿Estela? she queries the frightened girl.

When the girl doesn't answer, Antonia tries again in a softer voice she might use on a frightened child. The girl hides her face in her hands, a silent weeping, not the dramatic wails of Tilly and Mona. ¿Eres Estela?

The girl offers the slightest nod, her voice muffled, so it's difficult to make out what she is saying. Something about having no one, no place to go. Es que estoy sola.

How can she be all alone in the world, when the boyfriend just moved heaven and earth to bring her all the way from Colorado to Vermont?

Tienes a Mario, Antonia reminds her. But the mention of her boyfriend brings on a new round of weeping, this time louder.

Antonia approaches slowly, concerned that the frightened girl might bolt. Nothing to be afraid of. It's not a crime to be lonely. Ya, ya, she soothes, reaching out her hand.

FIVE

Dar a luz

Once indoors, Antonia can see that Estela is still a girl on the cusp of womanhood. In fact, if hers had been a family of means back home, she'd probably be having her quinceañera, instead of getting herself in trouble with a boyfriend headed out of the country. Her face has a sweet, girlish roundness; her eyes, an astonishment that gives a child's tug to the heart. She's actually quite pretty, her brown skin so smooth and unblemished it looks polished. Antonia catches herself doing one of those Third-to-First-World makeovers she deplores in others: put on a little makeup, give her a nice haircut, dress her up in some trendy clothes, and Estela could be a model in one of those diversity-touting brands—the only problem again being the deplorable condition of her teeth, a few missing, one incisor that looks eaten away by what appears to be decay.

¿Quieres algo de comer? Antonia offers. Not that there's much in the house, as she had emptied the fridge and pantry of perishables when she left. Salsa and parmesan on crackers, for the main course; for dessert, the same crackers with Nutella—which she used to stock up on, as it was a favorite of Sam's, all but the opened jar having gone to the local food pantry.

Just water, Estela says, downing a first glass, then a refill. After the desert crossing, she probably can't get enough of it.

Antonia is aching to know what happened next door. Did Roger throw the girl off the farm when her week of grace was up? If so, what are Mario's plans? But an ingrained sense of courtesy kicks in. When she taught *The Odyssey*, Antonia would point out to her students how being a host involved certain protocols: before all else, there was the greeting, the foot washing, the feeding. Only after the guest had been properly attended to came the payback: tell me your story.

One urgent question she does allow herself to ask Estela now. ¿Cuándo vas a dar a luz?

The girl looks at her blankly. Dar a luz, Antonia repeats. Do they say it differently in Mexico? When is the baby due? She gestures a round belly, then turns her palms out.

The girl shrugs. Could it be she doesn't know? Has no one taught her the science of her own body? But then, why does she look so worried? Perhaps she does understand but is afraid of giving a wrong answer.

It's going to be soon enough, that much Antonia can tell. She'll have to call the Open Door Clinic for an appointment as well as check on the hospital's policy if the girl goes into labor. Would Admissions have to notify the authorities? Would Estela be rushed back across the border before the baby drops anchor stateside? How does that all work?

That's for Mario to figure out, she reminds herself.

But he doesn't have the language or know-how to negotiate the medical bureaucracy, which has eluded Antonia herself since she went on Medicare. *The entrails of the health care system*, a phrase she has come to associate with the whole dysfunctional federal government, a stinky coil of stomach, small intestine, bowel (the three branches), none of them working properly.

There's always Mama Terry, though Mario would have to come up with some cash to pay for her services.

Recently, several ad hoc migrant groups have sprung up around the state with a phone tree of volunteers who can translate, offer rides. Antonia somehow got put on that list. Just because she's Latina doesn't automatically confer on her the personality or inclinations of a Mother Teresa. It irritates her, this moral profiling based on her ethnicity. Forget *The Odyssey* and the tradition of harboring strangers. When is Mario coming by? Antonia blurts out.

Estela winces. Antonia has touched a sore spot. I don't know, Estela says in a whisper.

How can she not know? Don't parting lovers always arrange for their next rendezvous? Unless, of course, those parting lovers don't have the luxury of controlling their lives. Or thinking they can.

Little by little the girl explains the fix she is in. She was not evicted by el patrón. It's Mario who wants nothing to do with her. It turns out Mario has been gone almost two years, first Tejas, then Carolina del Norte, finally settling in Vermont this past January. No way el bebé is his. (So, she does know her science.) When Estela arrived with that big belly of hers, he was as surprised as Antonia. Furious Estela had not told him.

But he wouldn't have let me come if I had told him, the girl is quick to add. He says so himself: he is not going to raise another man's bastard.

But it's not your fault, Antonia defends the girl. Antonia has been following reports on the news: girls traveling to the border, raped by coyotes, by those who run the so-called safe houses, by thieves, thugs, even by other migrants. But when Estela doesn't jump to her own defense, Antonia asks as delicately as possible, not wanting, God knows, to stir up any dragons. ¿Te violaron?

Estela bows her head in shame.

Dímelo. Tell me your story.

Sobbing, Estela confesses. She was not sure Mario was ever coming back. She was lonely. There was a man in her village, un hombre importante. He paid her attention, bought her pretty things, gave her money for her mother and younger siblings. We are seven sisters, she explains. No brothers.

Seven sisters! We are—Antonia stops herself. Is it still four sisters? She shakes away the horrible thought. It's been a respite from that horror to have to attend to someone else's horror.

Estela goes on to recount that when she became pregnant, the important man wanted her gone. He had a wife, his honor to protect. He found a coyote and paid for Estela's journey.

But wait, I thought Mario paid for the trip? He borrowed a bunch of money.

That was after the robbery. The first coyote abandoned Estela's group in the desert, after stealing from
them all they carried; Estela ended up in the hands of
a second coyote, and that's when Mario stepped in to
help. He only knew that Estela was en route to him. Had
she told Mario then about her condition, what would
have become of her, of her baby?

This is telenovela material—in fact, some critics
would say, Too much, ratchet it down a notch. But it
isn't a telenovela to the people it happens to. Another
way to dismiss their plight. Ratchet it down a notch.

I will talk with Mario, Antonia promises.

The girl's face lights up. Tell him I want to be with
him; tell him I didn't know what else to do.

Desperate situations call for desperate moves,
Mario should understand. But for the obfuscations of
machismo—Antonia's own father banished first one,
then another daughter when he discovered they had
transgressed with their American boyfriends. Antonia's
exile came spring of her senior year at college: her father
called her dorm one Saturday only to find out from the
big mouth at the switchboard that Antonia was away
for the weekend with her boyfriend. When she returned,
there were half a dozen pink message slips tacked to
her door, *Call home.* Her father answered on the first

ring, shouting into the mouthpiece, YOU ARE DEAD TO ME.

A year later, Antonia showed up at her parents' house in Queens. Her boyfriend had left her; she had lost her job, working the night shift at the state mental facility, her charges tied to their beds—the days before patients' rights and HIPAA monitoring of conditions. Nights were surreal, filled with howling, screams, shrieks, wails. The distraught and disturbed in need of soothing. The soiled in need of a cleanup. And here Antonia had taken the night shift thinking she'd get a lot of writing done. When she complained to her supervisor about the patients' mistreatment, she was fired. Where could she go? She hitchhiked home. Only then, when she had hit rock bottom, did her father "forgive her."

But along with machismo, the culture also commands respect for elders. Antonia is now la doñita. Older than Mario's mother by a dozen years. She will counsel him on the right way to act in this situation.

Gracias, gracias, ay, gracias, the girl keeps saying, tears in her eyes.

Wait to thank me till it's over, Antonia jokes. She feels uneasy accepting Estela's gratitude when she knows damn well she'd rather pass on this heavy load.

* * *

AFTER SETTLING ESTELA into the guest room, Antonia heads for next door. She turns into the driveway—Roger's pickup is gone—and parks in front of the trailer behind the barn. The curtains the workers always keep drawn lift ever so slightly. Before she can even knock, the door opens: José comes out on the concrete stoop, then steps down to the ground to stand eye level with her.

Mario no está, he announces.

Mario not here? ¡Por favor! she challenges the nervous young man. It's not like the undocumented have the freedom to go missing or for a leisurely stroll in this predominately white town and state. Her minority students often complained to Antonia about being followed around in stores, as if the darker color of their skin made them likely shoplifters. Migrant justice groups have taken up the issue: immigration control is not supposed to be the province of local law enforcement. Some enlightened counties—like her own—have outright refused to be an arm of ICE. But that doesn't guarantee a damn thing; a disgruntled state trooper or a cop in a bad mood after his wife left him or after he nicked himself shaving can always phone in an anonymous tip. Alerts are constantly issued—somehow Antonia got herself on that email list, too: *La migra picked up two outside Walmart in Burlington; ICE arrested three passengers*

getting off a bus. La policía stopped a car about a bro-
ken taillight and apprehended three individuals, a col-
lege girl transporting two undocumented migrants. The
student was taking them out for pizza, first time off the
farm in months the day after Thanksgiving—jeez, Black
Friday all right—and the three were brought to the local
jail: the student was later released, a hearing pending; the
two young men kept behind bars, soon to be deported.

No me voy hasta que no lo vea, Antonia announces,
loud enough for Mario to hear her on the other side of
the thin door. She is not leaving until she talks to him.

Okay, okay, José concedes, looking over his shoulder.
He reminds Antonia of a teenager covering for a buddy
in hot water. Mario is somewhere on the farm; José is
not sure where. We don't want any trouble. La doñita
knows how difficult el patrón can be.

I can be difficult, too. Antonia stands her ground,
one hand on her hip, a cultural signal if there ever was
one that this viejita means business. Mario! she calls out,
her voice in command mode. Mario!

How different her behavior at this moment from her
docility in the Illinois station with Officer Morgan. Sam
often noted that Antonia got a lot bossier in Spanish.
The minute they touched ground in the DR, a more self-
assured self took over. But in English, even after years of

education and employment, the worm of self-doubt still eats away at the core of her certainties.

The trailer door finally opens a crack. Déjala entrar, Mario calls to José. Soon el patrón will be back from his errand, and he has already told them in a loud voice, as if the issue is volume not language: NO VISITORS. Visitors spell trouble. Roger's illegal aliens are his own dirty little secret. He doesn't relish breaking the law but sometimes even law-abiding citizens have to defy the authorities in order to survive. Desperate situations call for desperate moves. Not so different, after all, from the undocumented he employs. Antonia was at that debate on campus a few months ago, farmers and their workers, talking about the similar predicaments they were in.

Inside the trailer, Antonia tries to persuade Mario. Estela's just a girl. She's got nowhere to go. And no, I can't keep her with me, she adds. You're going to have to figure something out.

Mario studies the scuffed linoleum floor as if it were a road map that might show him a way out of his dilemma. Antonia knows he's in the unenviable position of not wanting to contradict la doñita: she could turn him in; she could complain to el patrón. But he can't get past his revulsion at taking up with a girl who willingly gave herself to another man. He has his own honor as a man to defend, he says.

Honor, schmonor. Antonia waves the word away. What about showing a little compassion? Estela made a stupid choice, but it was only because she was lonely. She thought she had lost you. She loves you. It's you she wants to be with.

Then she shouldn't have done what she did. He had to make many sacrifices himself. It took him a while to cross over, to pay back the money he'd borrowed to pay the coyotes so he had something to send home. Even then, he had been against her making the journey north, precisely because he did not want her exposed to any harm. But it turns out, she had already willfully thrown away the flower of her girlhood.

Antonia is surprised by the fanciful phrase coming from the mouth of this impoverished and uneducated man. As if poetry can't survive in such impoverished conditions. In fact, poetry (and honor) might be all you do have. Sometimes she catches a glimpse of her faulty default self, and she doesn't like what she sees. We all make mistakes, she reminds Mario more gently. Look at Jesus, didn't he teach us to forgive? Perdónanos nuestras deudas, así como nosotros perdonamos a nuestros deudores, she intones. Forgive us our trespasses. How readily she recalls the words of her childhood prayers. Bedrock stuff she'll never get rid of. Madre Teresa, after all.

But Mario's bedrock machismo has an equally strong hold. He shakes his head in quick jabs. He will have nothing to do with esa puta. Take her to the migra and they will send her back home, where she belongs.

Don't call her that! Antonia feels her own anger rising. She's not a puta. She's . . . una jovencita, loca enamorada . . . Antonia struggles for the correct term, convinced if she lands on the right phrasing, it will be the abracadabra that unlocks the young man's heart. But she's fallen out of practice of arguing her case in Spanish now that Mami and Papi are gone.

Call her what you want, Mario says, a snarky insolence in his voice Antonia has never heard before. It grants her a rare glimpse of who the young man might be in a world where he could be the macho, wielding power. But to me she is no better than a prostitute.

José has been standing by, witnessing the escalating scene. He comes forward now. El patrón is due back any moment. If la doñita will allow him, he, José, will talk to Mario, convince him of the honorable thing to do even if the girl has done a dishonorable thing. ¿Hasta mañana?

Antonia is relieved to defer the confrontation till tomorrow. She needs to run into town, get a few groceries, connect with her sisters over what has or hasn't transpired with Izzy. Has Investigator Kempowski come up with anything? Has Mona landed in Boston? Tilly set out from home? She also needs to make those calls to the clinic and the hospital.

The last thing she needs . . . She doesn't dare complete the thought. Just thinking it might bring on the next worst thing.

ON HER WAY into town, Antonia calls her sisters, using the Bluetooth device Sam recently installed in her car, knowing how Antonia liked to use her driving time to make many of her obligatory calls. I don't want to end up being a widower, he had remarked. Those now seemingly prescient moments come back to haunt her: the past signaling this future, but with the roles reversed.

Tilly's number, then Mona's, goes to voicemail after half a dozen rings. Do they hear church bells and decide not to pick up? *Any news? Please call me back*. She dials Izzy. Why not? Instantly, she's shunted to voicemail, Izzy's phone out of juice or turned off.

Kempowski also can't come to the phone right now, but her call is important to him. Please leave a detailed message. She decides not to, as there's only so much nagging you can do, even if you are paying someone a hefty fee to find your missing sister. Besides, she wants to talk to him in real time, another strange phrase, *real time*. What other kind of time is there? Language seems increasingly strange. When did that start?

She's in the checkout line when a call comes in from Mona. She landed a couple of hours ago at Logan, where she was picked up by Maritza, and they're headed to Athol. Some interesting details have been surfacing. Maritza saw Izzy a couple of days before Izzy left to look at some properties for her centro. Izzy was high as a kite, talking nonstop. At one point Maritza said Izzy went to the bathroom, and her cell started to ring, so Maritza opened Izzy's handbag to answer it, and *whoa*! It was full of cash, packets of bills, and half a dozen bottles of medications. So, did you rob a bank? Or a drugstore? Maritza confronted Izzy when she came back to their table. Izzy just narrowed her eyes and grinned with mischief. I mean, just the idea that Izzy would be walking around with a bag full of loot.

Kempowski needs to know all this.

I've already told him, Mona informs her. There's a gloating tone to baby sister's voice. As the youngest, she loves it when she can be first one to know and then report to the others.

Antonia unloads her cart onto the conveyor belt, a pile of groceries she would never buy for herself. But back in aisle two amid the sugary cereals, Antonia decided to bend her strict eat-healthy rules to accommodate Estela. Cocoa puffs, potato chips, Oreos, soda, taco shells, Goya beans, cheddar cheese, chocolate milk. The items speed forward into the ready hands of *Hi, I'm Haley*.

Hold on a sec, Antonia tells Mona. Haley needs to know if Antonia wants paper or plastic. Antonia hoists her paper bags into the cart and rolls away from all the noise.

Sounds like you bought up the store, Mona says, sounding offended about having to wait.

Does she tell Mona about what has come up? Antonia decides not to. Last thing she needs is Mona's advice about what to do with Estela.

Anyhow, as I was saying, I called Kempowski, and he already was in touch with the Realtor, Nancy Something, who couldn't say enough nice things about Izzy, how she, Nancy, felt she had met a long-lost sister. How she showed Izzy some really great deals. But for now we're just going with the motel and the farm. Mona has moved from recounting what she has learned about the Realtor to imitating her.

A farm! Antonia feels she's trapped in the maze that is Izzy's mind in one of her manic spells. The world is crazy, grant it that, and granted she has been so wrapped up in her grief, but still, how could its craziness have come so close and she never noticed until recently? She needs the psychic version of Sam's movement lights to flash warnings in her brain when precarious situations and needy people are nearby.

Mona, too, has lost her glee. She continues her narrative in a weary voice. How Izzy slept over at Realtor Nancy's house before taking off to visit her sisters outside Chicago. How Nancy tucked her in that night. Her "long-lost sister" on whom she can unload all her worthless properties. What a total jerk! I don't even want to talk to that woman, Mona says in their mother's ultimatum voice.

We're going to have to work with a lot of jerks if we want to find our sister, Antonia reminds Mona. She, too, is finding it increasingly difficult to keep up her faith in people, in herself. In the past when her own stash got this low, there was always Sam filling up her cup with his abundant kindness. She has continued to think a lot about the afterlife, especially in the absence of any sign from Sam. What, if anything, does it mean? An afterlife? All she has come up with is that the only way not to let the people she loves die forever is to embody what she loved about them. Otherwise the world is indeed depleted. Sam: always thinking the best of people. Izzy: casting her bread upon the waters. Generosities of which

Antonia was often the lucky recipient. But what is she thinking? Izzy is not dead.

And guess what? Mona interrupts Antonia's thoughts. Kempowski was going to have Izzy's cell phone pinged, but no need. Nancy turned it in. Seems Izzy left it behind there and it ran out of juice. No wonder we couldn't reach her.

Tomorrow, Mona and Maritza will be meeting up with a local investigator that Kempowski has enlisted near Athol. They mean to stay there for a few days, looking around, talking to this Realtor Nancy. I've changed my flight home. You want to come down and meet us? Mona asks. A question with a strong-arm muscle of *should* in it.

Antonia explains the situation that has come up, burnishing the bleak details, as Mona isn't making any empathic sounds at her end. But Mona is stern in her response: sisterhood comes first. Izzy is their sister. So as not to sound heartless, she adds that it is very sad of course about the girl, but Antonia shouldn't get in the middle of a boyfriend-girlfriend fight.

It's not a fight. He threw her out. She's homeless, helpless.

A long silence at the other end. Do what you want, Mona says in an aggrieved voice.

Neither alternative is what Antonia wants. What is the right thing to do? An old quandary, and the older she gets, the more she realizes she still hasn't figured it out. Tolstoy had it right in that story she used to teach about the three questions: What is the best time to do things? Who is the most important one? What is the right thing to do? Funny how Antonia remembers the questions but can't for the life of her remember if Tolstoy provided any answers.

Let me see what I can work out, Antonia promises, already making a mental list: check in on José's man-to-man talk with Mario, set up medical care for Estela, and housing, if she can't convince Roger about an extension of his kindness. Because no, Antonia's home is not an option. She has already decided: *she* is the most important one.

BACK AT THE HOUSE, Estela is fast asleep in the guest room. She must be bone tired, pobrecita. Antonia had shown the girl the room, laid out some towels. Why don't you freshen up, get some rest? I'll be back in a little while. The towels are still in their neat pile, Estela on top of the made bed, her head cushioned on one arm, a red string bracelet matching Mario's on her left wrist. Maybe there's an expiration date on how much luck and protection it can provide?

Antonia takes the folded blanket and covers the girl, who startles awake but, on hearing the soothing Ya, ya, duérmete, duérmete, instantly falls back to sleep.

When Mona was recounting how Realtor Nancy tucked in Izzy, Antonia had felt uneasy, as if her sister were being fattened up, not for the kill, but for the sell, an abandoned motel and a farm in the middle of nowhere. But now there's a tenderness to the thought. Whatever has happened to Izzy, she did experience the kindness of a host toward a stranger.

Later, at her laptop, recalling Estela's blank look, Antonia Googles the Spanish for giving birth, *dar a luz*. Is it not used in Mexico? According to one of the websites, *parir* is the working-class term. *Dar a luz* was used originally to refer to the Virgin Mary giving birth to the light of the world, a euphemism the upper classes appropriated, a more polite way of referring to a lady's parturition. Antonia had often bragged to Sam about the poetry of her native language, the beautiful way, for example, that Spanish had of referring to giving birth: dar a luz, "give to the light." That intense need to get the words right.

But even the beauties of language, of words rightly chosen, are riddled with who we are, class and race, and whatever else will keep us—so we think—safe on the narrow path.

SIX

Who is the most important one?

Strange dreams, but then, aren't they all? The mishmash of facts, the time travel, the faces shifting into each other. A taste of the afterlife? In tonight's dream, Antonia is about to give birth. A surprise since she has never been pregnant, not to mention she is definitely postmenopausal. Of such stuff are dreams made. Sam, however, is not surprised. He is driving her to the hospital. As they climb up the snowy pass, he loses control of the car; they plunge over the side of the mountain, but then, miraculously, the car comes to an abrupt stop, held back by a row of trees.

You stay here, Sam orders, self-assured even in *her* dreams. I'll go get help. Be right back.

Hours go by. Then, somehow (the beloved adverb of dreams) Antonia is at a police station reporting Samuel Sawyer as a missing person and almost immediately the scene changes and she is at the hospital again, in labor. A nurse is at the door, saying Knock-knock, instead of knocking.

Están tocando la puerta, a voice whispers urgently.

Antonia stirs awake. A big-bellied, frightened girl bends over her. The real-time story coheres: homeless Estela, her fatherless child, the talk with Mario this morning, Mona waiting for her in Massachusetts, Tilly on her way—the to-do list of the day ahead.

¿Quién es? she asks Estela, as if the girl would know anyone in Vermont besides Mario, José, and el patrón next door.

No sé, Estela answers, glancing around the room, looking for a place to hide.

The knocking persists. Who could it be at her door this early in the morning? Antonia checks her alarm clock to corroborate the exact hour of her grievance. Eight already! She must have overslept. She scrambles out of bed, hoping it's not Mario. He knows better than to stand conspicuously at the front door in view of the road. More likely he'd come around and knock on a back window now that he knows the layout of the house.

Antonia throws on one of Sam's old work shirts over her nightgown. Estela is to go back to her room— Antonia's already calling it "your room." Close the door. No salgas por ninguna razón. Here she is whispering in her own house.

The girl dashes off, amazing how deft she is with that big belly. But then, Antonia reminds herself, Estela also crossed a desert with that belly. How could the coyote have agreed to take her on? He must have already known he'd be robbing the group, abandoning them in the middle of nowhere.

Some people must never ask themselves, What is the right thing to do? Or if they do, they phrase the question differently: What is the right thing to do that will guarantee I am the one in command, the one you fear, the one who gets to answer the three questions?

As she approaches the entryway, Antonia cannot make out the face through the frosted panel alongside the door—a looming shadow, someone tall, confident, with a persistent, declarative knock. Sam? she almost asks.

Who is it? she calls out before looking through the peephole.

Sheriff Boyer.

Her heart sinks. Has he come to search her house? Can he do that? Wouldn't he need a warrant? She opens the door a crack, playing it up: a woman intruded upon, a woman who just woke up, clutching the work shirt closed, running her hand through her loose hair, so the man feels awkward, invading an intimate female space. I overslept, just woke up. How can I help you, Sheriff?

Sorry about that, ma'am. He touches his hat, furtively checking her out, the bit of nightgown showing under the shirt, his eye lingering just a hair's breadth of a moment at her neckline; she is not yet so old that the uniformed man only a few years younger than she wouldn't still notice the dip of cleavage, the suggestive roundness. Her hand flies to her neck, another performed gesture of modesty.

You okay? he asks, no clue yet as to why he is here in the first place.

I'm okay. I mean—does she play up that she is recently widowed? The grief card, someone described it in a grieving chatroom Antonia hit upon. *What weird card game are you playing with your loss?* Antonia wondered.

Is something wrong, Sheriff?

A neighbor reported seeing someone coming in and out of your garage. You've been away, they said.

What neighbor would that be? No one lives directly beside or in front of her; all the houses are staggered and separated by an acre or more, except for the cluster toward the end of the road. Perhaps the report was by one of those neighbors. Mrs. Gaudet? The cranky lady in the cardigan? Unlikely it would be Roger. Given his work crew, he wouldn't want cops patrolling the road. She assures Sheriff Boyer that all is well. I'd ask you in but—she glances down at herself, still in her nightgown, her feet bare.

No need for that, he says, peering over her shoulder. Antonia wills herself not to turn and check, betraying her guilt. You mind, though, if I take a look in your garage?

A slight hesitation, before she says, not at all. Let me open it for you. Hold on a sec while I put on my shoes. She closes the door, hurries through the mudroom into the garage, casts a look around, stacks the cushions back in a pile, a last glance, before she presses the button and the door lifts on Sheriff Boyer. He grins at the sight of her and again touches his hat in salutation. Ma'am, he repeats. The way he says it, in that low syrupy voice, it almost sounds sexy, better, at any rate, than "Mrs. Sawyer," as most people in town refer to her.

She watches his assessing gaze. Sorry about the mess, she says, as if this were her living room and he an honored guest.

You should see mine, he says, chuckling.

I haven't kept up much since my husband's passing. With this set of folks, the same subset with whom she feels she can allude to Jesus, she uses the term *passing*, death no more than a lane on a highway, for those speeding into the unknown.

Sorry for your loss, he says genuinely, one hand actually flying up to his heart. That Dr. Sawyer was a good man. Took care of my mother's glaucoma. Yours truly, too. I called him up one Sunday afternoon, a thistle in my eye, and he had me drive over to his office, took it right out, didn't charge a red cent.

That, more than the sheriff donation sticker, probably kept the Sawyers safe from speeding tickets.

Sounds like Sam all right, Antonia says wistfully. Then, too apropos not to add: he was the good cop to my bad cop.

Oh, I don't know about that, the sheriff wags his head. You're a pretty nice lady yourself. The freckles on his face sharpen. Ruddy-faced, big-chested, he looks good in that hat. Cowboyish and kind.

He has stepped inside the garage, peering into the corners, circling back to face her, nothing seems to have caught his eye that she can tell. Sorry to disturb you, he concludes.

Can I ask who reported the intruder?

You can, he concedes the point, but it's me who can't say. He looks away, not wanting to see the disappointment on her face. Let's just say some people have nothing better to do than keep an eye on everyone else. He chuckles—a verb coined for his type of avuncular laughter.

Stay safe, he says for good-bye, and starts walking away, but then pivots, pulls out his wallet from his back pocket, and hands her his card. You see anything worrisome, anything, you give us a call. We'll be right over. The civil servant's royal *we*.

The card has a sheriff-star logo in soft focus, the contact information in sharp, black no-nonsense print. On the back, his handwritten extension.

Thank you, Sheriff. I'll be okay. What she tells everybody. *The best thing you can give the people who love you is to take care of yourself so you don't become a burden on them.*

Who is the most important one? Myself, myself, myself. Maybe Izzy decided on the second best thing: to disappear altogether from the isolation of self-care.

FEELING MORE URGENCY after the sheriff's visit, Antonia heads next door to talk to Mario and José. She needs to make arrangements for Estela before she takes off for Massachusetts. She is getting out of her car when she runs into Roger, scowling as he comes back from the barn. Already a bad day and it's only just begun.

Hey there, she says with the cheerful lilt of a kindergarten teacher. She launches into her story. A family emergency. A sister gone missing. The remaining sisters are convening in Western Mass, where the missing sister was last seen. We're going to try to track her down.

Roger must be wondering why she's giving him more information than he needs, front-loading, as it were, before she appends her request: Can Roger let Mario's girlfriend (no need to go into details) stay another week?

Roger's eyes narrow, studying her. Someone's not telling the truth here. Last I heard, they broke up.

Antonia's head seesaws, yes and no. Actually, it's a bit more complicated, she responds.

Roger's got a hundred and forty cows to milk and a back field to spray with liquid manure. He has no time for complications. Just answer the question, the TV judges instruct the gabby accused person on the witness stand. A yes or a no. So, is this the afterlife? Everything black or white? A heavenly court with St. Peter as judge. Yes or no. No complications.

Please, Antonia pleads. She knows she's making a nuisance of herself, after resolving not to become a burden on anyone.

Roger lets out a sigh as if to expel some offending foreign matter. Is he asking himself, *What is the right thing to do?*

If the fellow wants to let her stay in the trailer, I don't know about it.

Thank you, oh thank you, Antonia gushes, as if Roger has agreed to far more than just turning a blind eye to a girl in trouble.

Roger glances over her shoulder; his scowl deepens. She turns to see José and Mario walking back to their trailer on a break from their morning chores. They stop at the sight of el patrón and la doñita talking. Instead of approaching, they wait deferentially to know the wishes of those in control.

It's power Antonia doesn't want. Never has. As a young woman, she dreaded getting her driver's license: suddenly having control of four thousand pounds of steel and rubber and glass. A tremendous jump from her featherweight ninety-five pounds. She used to suffer from panic attacks those first few months after getting her license. She still feels anxious behind the wheel. I hate having power, Antonia would often say to Sam. But Sam didn't buy her disclaimers. How about the power of being able to use words? Or being a teacher running a classroom? How about your power over me? And your beauty, he added, deflecting her defensiveness with a compliment. Beautiful women have that power over men.

She was hardly a beauty even as a young woman and definitely not as the middle-aged one he had met and married. But she was not about to accuse him of blindness when what he was seeing was delightfully in her favor.

Antonia signals to the two men to join them. She explains that el patrón is going to let Estela stay in the trailer until Antonia can get back from a family emergency. I'll bring her over before I leave, Antonia adds. Mario stares at her in disbelief. Has she suffered total amnesia and forgotten his views from the day before? Did José talk with Mario, asking him to reconsider whether his honor would allow for forgiveness? Doesn't she want to hear if Mario agreed?

No, not really. Antonia doesn't have time to indulge agency, rights, agreements. She is the one with the power to say how their story will go. She does not return his gaze. She has rendered him invisible, like everyone else. Not something she would want to fess up to in that book of hers.

On the short drive back to her house, Antonia defends herself, pleading her case before the stern internal judge who, instead of a puritanical white-powdered wig, wears her mother's face. Not surprisingly, Judge Mami often rules against her.

How much power does Antonia really have? Talk about powerless! She has lost her husband; her sister is missing. And behind these untimely losses, the timely ones, the whole flank of buffering elders, parents, tías, tíos, who have died in the natural progression of things, but still, natural or not, they leave behind holes in the heart, places of leakage where Antonia feels the depletion of spirit, the slow bleed of chronic grieving. Language used to be good at stanching the flow, the intense—call it desperate—need to get the words just right. But more and more words are inadequate . . . a *raid on the inarticulate with shabby equipment*, the poet wrote about writing, his lines showing no signs of inadequacy.

Antonia has had enough! Again she thinks of Job. Except for the skin disease, the dead cattle and kids, she could be Job, waiting for the other shoe to drop. What more will be asked of her? That is a stupid, stupid question, she tells herself in order to shame herself into acceptance. Just like God did to Job. But she is not God. Still, she doesn't know any better than to dumbly, bluntly keep asking herself that question.

* * *

LIKE ANY LOVER with a go-between, Estela wants to know every detail of Antonia's meeting with Mario: What did he say? What did la doñita respond? How did he seem about the baby?

It's all good, Antonia lies. A favorite phrase of her students, a polite way of saying, back off.

But even after being reassured, Estela looks dubious. What if Mario changes his mind again? Estela recounts how she ended up in la doñita's garage. Mario got drunk. He told her he was sending her back. She ran away. More of the story than Antonia would like to know—if she plans to get away at all.

I'll talk to him and to José. What else can she do?

Go take a warm bath, she instructs the girl. I'll put together some things for you.

Estela nods, the obedient girl who will not be straying from the narrow path again anytime soon.

Antonia calls the Open Door Clinic to set up an appointment. The receptionist greets her warmly. We've missed you, but no worries. The clinic has hooked up with the college's Spanish department. An internship for double majors (Spanish and premed)—they come over to translate. The news momentarily appeases Antonia's guilt. No need to feel it's either her or the dragons. One of the easements of the First World, there's always an organization or agency to pick up the slack. A passing of the moral buck. But what will this do over time to her sense of compassion?

It just so happens that the doctor in attendance tonight is Dr. Trotter, Sam's colleague, whom Antonia has met on a number of social occasions. She's okay, was Sam's lukewarm assessment, perhaps unfairly based on Beth's appearance: overweight, often out of breath—a not-so-good advertisement for the medical profession. But Beth is a kind soul who will go out of her way to help.

I feel awful, Beth confesses when she comes to the phone. She has been meaning to be in touch with Antonia, that's why she took the call tonight when she heard it was Sam Sawyer's widow. Sam was such a generous mentor to so many of his younger colleagues, including Beth. Anything she can do?

Antonia recounts the situation: the undocumented teenager about to give birth, the disgruntled boyfriend, the farmer's short window of welcome.

Beth is full of sighs—or maybe it's just her shortness of breath. Her first, I assume? Beth queries.

I think so, Antonia conjectures. So much she doesn't know about Estela. The girl did show Antonia her birth certificate—she's actually seventeen, looks no older than fifteen—and a primary school ID, the same sweet, round face, with two tidy beribboned braids rather than the single one down her back.

A perfect storm all right, Beth sums up after hearing all the details. And of course, she'll arrange a ride for the girl to be brought to her practice for a prelabor checkup. She'll also alert the ER and Admissions over at the hospital to notify her directly if a young Mexican mom in labor is brought in. And here's her cell number in case Antonia should need to reach her directly.

In a matter of minutes, Estela is set up with a safety net of options. These are lucky breaks, courtesy of Sam's practicing in a small Vermont town for over forty years. Antonia, and by association, Estela, can tap this network, bypassing those entrails of the medical care system. Theirs is still a small-town hospital with a handful of satellite practitioners. But change is on the horizon. Soon the tiny hospital will go the way of the one-room schoolhouse. The large medical center up in Burlington will be taking over the hospital and satellite practices this summer. Their CEO has been issuing reassuring bulletins: NOTHING WILL CHANGE. YOU WILL STILL BE ABLE TO . . . The notices posted in every office and examining room. We shall see; Antonia tries to stave off her cynicism. But it is, after all, the nature of the corporate beast to gobble up small fry without noticing at all, ensconced as it is in the upper floors of an office building with picture-window views of Lake Champlain, far from the madding crowd of faces on the street, in grocery stores, waiting rooms, the P.O., the co-op, as well as invisible ones who increasingly enter Antonia's line of vision and become visible: Estela, José, Mario with a bloody cut in his right palm from the blade of the saw. Even the hulking sheriff with a thistle hooked into a burning eye will soon not have the option of being examined gratis by a kind doctor on his own time but will first have to undergo a formal admission at the ER, a plastic bracelet affixed to his wrist, his information typed into the system, an electronic trail leading directly to that wallet in his back pocket.

Antonia fills a satchel with things Estela might need in the days ahead, next door or at the hospital, if she gives birth before Antonia gets back—what Antonia is hoping for: let someone else take over the problem that has knocked on her door. It's unlikely that Mario and José will have extra sheets, towels, blankets, or that Roger will come over with a welcome basket of bath soap, shampoo, conditioner. Do men even use conditioner? Sam never did, but then his hair had gotten so thin. What was there to condition? A hair brush, deodorant, baby oil,

hand lotion—what to offer an impoverished teenager
on the verge of labor? She recalls how Sam's church,
a liberal, well-intended congregation, put together care
bags for him and Antonia to distribute when they next
went down to the Dominican Republic. In addition to
Antonia's practical suggestions, donors included products Antonia had never used herself—backscratchers,
exfoliant foot peel, vitamin boosters made from natural
products. Once, a can of feminine hygiene spray, whose
function Antonia deduced from reading the instructions.

Strange bread people cast upon another's needy
waters.

ON THE DRIVE OVER, Estela is full of questions. When
will Antonia be back? Where is Massachusetts? ¿Cómo
se dice *vaca, árbol, sol, nube, conejo, estrella*? ¿Cómo se
dice *parir, me duele, tengo hambre, tengo miedo*? This
sudden endearing need to get the words right in English.
Cow, tree, sun, cloud, rabbit, star. The barking-dog ringtone goes off, startling the girl, who looks around the
car for el perro. Antonia laughs. It's just my sister calling. ¿Cómo se dice *ringtone* in Spanish? Antonia pulls
over, as they're almost at Roger's and she doesn't want
to sit in his driveway talking. She has been waiting for
Mona to call back or text with the exact meeting point

in Western Mass. She plans to set out after delivering her cargo.

Mona has met with Realtor Nancy. She's super nervous, like she's hiding something. A pandemonium of barking breaks out in the background. Not her ringtone gone rogue. Has Mona flown her dogs up from North Carolina?

No, no, no. They're Maritza's labs, Mona says, annoyed that Antonia doesn't already know that her rescues sound nothing at all like that. Shades of Sam's annoyance when Antonia didn't automatically know the thoughts and feelings in *his* head.

As I was saying, Mona says, this woman is, like, totally creepy.

Creepy as in Unabomber creepy? Or just nerdy creepy? You think she's done something to Izzy?

The mango doth not fall far from the tree, Mona cackles, an expression the sisterhood has Latinized and loves to quote whenever one of them is acting like their mother. Mami Mango was the mother of all sleuths: always suspicious of their friends, figuring out their whereabouts, indiscretions, alibis, sniffing out their pot smoking, discovering their diaphragms, packets of birth control in their sock drawers. There wasn't a stranger Mami encountered after they arrived in the United States of los Locos de Remate that she didn't suspect of dubious motives. It wasn't as simple as gringo profiling. She was equally wary of her fellow Dominicans in exile.

What I think, Mona says after calming down the dog clamor, is that your sister might have paid a hefty cash deposit Nancy is hoping she won't have to return. Izzy also picked up an application for a loan at the local bank, a loan she's not likely to get. She told Nancy that, if all else fails, she'd borrow the money from her sisters.

How did Mona find out so much? Baby sister has only been a few hours on the ground. Antonia is filled with a grudging admiration for Mona's cunning and persistence. But Mona defers. A local investigator Kempowski uses for the Boston area has dug all this stuff up.

Mona reports that the same source found out Izzy closed her account at the bank before leaving Boston, to the tune of ten something grand. Must be the bundle that Maritza saw in Izzy's bag.

Izzy walking around with that kind of ready cash! Criminal bait to be sure. Even if no one mugs her, who knows how long it'll last her? How often did she say to attendants, waiters, Keep the change? Even times when the change was more than the price of the purchase or service she was paying for? On a visit last summer, Antonia and Sam took Izzy to the local farmer's market. A darling waif of a boy, no older than ten, with round glasses, freckles, and an icing-on-the-cake cowlick, was playing his violin, shoppers occasionally stopping to listen before unloading their quarters, at most a single dollar, into the instrument's case. Izzy stood enthralled, calling for encores, before tossing down a twenty. The boy's eyes widened with shock as a beaming Izzy shouted out BRAVO! at the top of her lungs.

He'll never be satisfied with less from now on, Sam muttered as they walked away. *Your* sister (here we go again, no one wanted Izzy on their relay team) always has to upstage everyone, even a kid playing his violin for mad money.

I don't think that's why she did it, Antonia defended Izzy, though Antonia herself couldn't figure out what motivated most of her sister's grand gestures. Was it some pathology, as Mona and Tilly believed, or a case of too large a spirit crammed inside too small a personality? As for Sam's disgruntled response, how much was it the good cop not liking to be upstaged by an even better cop?

Mona explains that she and Maritza are staying put in Athol. Moratorium on the jokes, okay? Mona announces, though she has been the one leading the charge in hilarity over the town's unfortunate name. Mona has found a great Airbnb with three bedrooms, dogs allowed, a jacuzzi—where they can all camp out while local law enforcement devote some of their resources to finding Izzy. Tilly is on her way, with Kaspar, who insisted on coming along. They are driving east, tracing what might have been Izzy's route, posting posters, talking to truckers. They'll meet up late tomorrow night or early the next morning and go from there.

So, there's really no urgency about Antonia's arrival. What's she going to do there that she can't do from home? The overreactions of the sisterhood, always in crisis, sounding the alarm, so exhausting any time, but particularly now when Antonia feels hollowed out.

You're the most American of us, her sisters have commented to Antonia in an accusatory tone. Just saying, they said smugly when she asked what was wrong with being whoever she was. Admittedly, she was the worrier, the insomniac, the most anxious and disciplined of the sisters. But it wasn't that she didn't feel as much as they did, but that she doled it out in limited portions. Of course, any such divergence from the culture of the sisterhood was considered a betrayal. So, for the last few years, she has been keeping her visits short and her interactions circumscribed.

Antonia considers coming up with some alibi, malingering for a few days before joining the fray. Not that staying home and dealing with the Estela-Mario predicament would be any picnic. But at least she'd delay days of escalating emotions, stewing in anxiety, listening to Mona and Tilly spout out conspiracy theories. *She* is the most important one. The selfish one who pulls away from the others, so sayeth the sisterhood. But now she's also the next in line, duty-bound to take care of her younger sisters.

I'm actually driving, Antonia explains. I pulled over to talk. Just text me the address, and I'll give you the heads-up when I'm on my way, okay?

Sure thing. Be careful. Love you. Reinstated into the sisterhood.

Love you, too.

Love you more, Mona says. Competing, even over who loves the others the most.

At the trailer, no one comes to the door in welcome, no one hurries down the steps to help carry in Estela's bag. Maybe the boys are cleaning up in preparation for their guest? Maybe they'll surprise her with female-ready digs? A cake, balloons?

Dream on. Antonia laughs at her wishful thinking.

Estela has been watching her closely. She doesn't

understand what's funny, but nonetheless, she smiles a tentative smile—on her face the eager look of a child wanting to please. Antonia feels a flush of protective tenderness.

You're going to be all right, she reassures the girl.

Once inside the trailer, Antonia is not so sure: Mario is grim and silent; José is all over himself, filling the silence with chatter; Estela, tentative, head bowed, her thank-yous barely audible. José shows the two women around: the tiny dirty kitchen, the dirty tiny bathroom, two tiny bedrooms—José has vacated his for Estela; he'll join Mario in the other one.

The time has come. Antonia pulls the worried girl to one side and slips an envelope into Estela's hands. It's my number and la doctora's and un dinerito. Anything . . . anything happens you go right next door to el patrón. The note explains what he's to do.

And then, she repeats again, you're going to be all right.

The young girl's lips tremble, tears well in her eyes. A child who has realized that her mother will not be staying with her on the first day of school.

I really have to go, Antonia pleads. She touches the red string on the girl's wrist. Acuérdate: you are armed with good luck. God will protect you. The tears fall.

Estela's crying is noiseless. Her sorrows aren't meant to disturb anyone.

But they disturb Antonia. The girl, the two boy-men, the world of impending doom in which they and others like them live. Antonia has veered from her narrow path. Looked over the guardrail at the reflection on the water below. As in a dream, faces shift into each other: Izzy's, Sam's, the face of the girl she is leaving behind, her own.

Who is the most important one?

SEVEN

Objects in mirror are closer than they appear

On her way to her sister rendezvous, Antonia can't stop thinking about Estela. Not just the immediate solution to the girl's problem, but what will become of this kid with a kid?

At the mountain pass, a car has pulled into the overlook area; a man and a woman are pointing out the landscape to each other. Never again will she do that with Sam. No matter the sips, the narrow path, grief keeps ambushing her: unsuspecting moments, nooks, crannies, cracks where the root system of loving is embedded in her life. Brutally yanked out with that tearing sound of detaching a clump of grass from the ground.

Antonia recognizes the very spot where in her recent dream she went off the road. No snow now, no icy patch sending her flying over the side of the mountain, no frost on the windshield. The trees are showing the faintest halo of green and gold. Spring, at last. Sam's favorite season.

She has been listening to a podcast. A therapist, recently widowed, is discussing her experience of loss and grieving. The woman is saying some wise things; in fact, she is quoting some of Antonia's own chestnuts—*in the midst of winter . . . an invincible summer. In a dark time, the eye begins to see*, and so on—but instead of feeling comforted, Antonia feels irritated. What is wrong with her? She listens to podcasts, reads books on grief, searches for answers to her questions. But any suggestions she is offered annoy her. She has already tried that—and guess what? It doesn't work.

The widowed therapist brings up Rilke. More chestnuts. *Love consists in this: that two solitudes protect, touch, and greet each other . . . Perhaps we are here in order to say: house, bridge, fountain . . .* Cómo se dice *parir, me duele, tengo hambre, tengo miedo*? (Estela intruding again.) In a letter to his good friend, a countess with too many surnames, Rilke has this wonderful insight, the therapist widow is saying. She doesn't want to mess it up. Give her a second to find the quote. The sound of turning pages and the woman reads, *Death does not wound us without, at the same time, lifting us toward a more perfect understanding of this being and of ourselves.*

Does Antonia really understand Sam any better now than she did before? Or herself? Perhaps with time she will. Everything is still too recent, though the year anniversary is fast approaching, the maximum she can ask of anyone's indulgence. Right now, she doesn't need to understand; she needs to stop the leakage of spirit, plug the hole in her heart.

She turns off the widow-therapist and plays a recording Izzy sent her recently. A medium who communicates with the dead. Izzy had gone to a group session in a large auditorium and the medium had picked her out of the audience—instantly endearing herself to their attention-hungry sister. Someone from the other side was trying to reach Izzy. Did the letter *M* mean anything to her? Mami? Izzy had offered up. Or, maybe, tío Manolo, a favorite uncle who succumbed to liver cancer? Then there's ex-husband Mark, diagnosed with a brain tumor, dead before the year was out. Or maybe it was Maritza, but wait, Maritza isn't dead. . .

Ay, Izzy, honey, that is the oldest trick! Does *M* mean

anything to you? the sisters mimicked and scoffed. A safe
bet when everyone in the world has to have a *m*other!

Why was Izzy messing around with this possibly
bogus new-agey evangelist-type character? The sisterhood put their heads together. The evangelist was Izzy's
kind of person. Someone who hung out at the fringes—
where Izzy went to cast her bread upon the waters, feed
the dragons. Seriously, did Izzy have any friends who
weren't going through or recovering from some trauma
or other? It's like if there's a fire, Izzy couldn't just stand
at a respectful distance and warm herself. Of course not.
How *borrrring*! *Watch this*! she'd howl, leaping into the
flames. Izzy needs help.

There was a simpler explanation, Antonia—the selfish one, the one to break off from the group conclusion—argued. Izzy was grieving the loss of their parents.
Yes, their deaths had been timely, Papi in his nineties,
Mami, mid-eighties. But Izzy had been left with no one
and nothing to fill the void. Until recently, when she
came up with her migrant-art-in-the-boonies scheme.
Antonia hadn't heard their sister this excited since . . .
since forever. Mona shook her head, exasperated with
Antonia's reluctance to accept that their sister has an
actual disease. Mona *does* have her MSW, in case anyone
in the family cares to notice. Antonia, meanwhile, has no

training in psychology and so wouldn't know. The highs are highs, but the crash is sure to come. Classic bipolar.

But Antonia keeps vacillating on what she thinks of Izzy's moods. Sometimes it seems that Izzy is just suffering from the chronic malaise that comes with being alive. *Even in Kyoto—* / *hearing the cuckoo's cry—* / *I long for Kyoto*, one of Antonia's favorite haikus and one she loves to quote to her sisters. We all have to make peace with that longing, learn to live with the holes in our hearts. It's the kind of remark that might have gone over well in her classes. But not with Mona and Tilly, who take her to task, Mona claiming that Antonia is in denial about the seriousness of their sister's illness, Tilly cursing her into compliance: Just go along with the fucking program for once!

Antonia has to defer to Mona's expertise. Still, it's a shame how every grand passion has been co-opted by some pathology or other. Indignation is now wounded narcissism. Outrage, an issue with anger management. Revenge, a post-traumatic stress disorder. These old-time passions only exist anymore in Russian novels and on stage, especially in the Met operas broadcast at the Town Hall Theatre. As Madame Butterfly stabs herself in despair or Desdemona spends her last virtuous breaths singing, the victim of Otello's jealous rage, Antonia weeps with abandon, embarrassed when the lights come up and she is surrounded by her dry-eyed fellow audience members. *Catharsis*, that's what she feels, a term she often used when teaching Greek tragedy to her students. Once again, she is reminded how much she misses them.

The medium on tape offers the kind of popularized consolations that would normally irritate Antonia, but instead she finds herself listening closely. How to recognize signs from your spirit loved ones. "Heaven winks," the medium calls them. You find a penny or a dime and the date on it means something. Antonia is always finding pennies, but she has never thought to check the date. You turn on the radio and your special song is playing. A stranger comes in your life and you find yourself responding not as you would but as your loved one would—

Antonia almost goes off the road when she hears this one.

Her former bad-cop self would have resisted getting involved with Estela's predicament. It isn't exactly that Antonia is hard-nosed; it's more that people get under her skin too easily—part of the problem. And right now, in her life, Antonia is operating so close to the bone, she has no surplus to throw upon needy waters.

But here she is already planning to call Estela this evening to check in. How are things going with Mario? How did the visit with la doctora go? It's almost hormonal—like a mother with her newborn—this pull toward this stranger. If she's not careful, Antonia's breasts will soon start flowing with milk—the milk of human kindness it would have to be! Her old-biddy titties have closed up shop. That, too, has crossed her mind. Will there be sex after Sam?

And what if there is no "after Sam"? If he's living *inside* her now? Much closer than she had imagined, like that warning on the side-view mirror reads: OBJECTS IN MIRROR ARE CLOSER THAN THEY APPEAR. Again, the seemingly ordinary phrase or random detail that offers life shape and meaning. *Hold through the silence*, the customer-service recording instructs her. A perfect meditation instruction! *Take in my give*, Mami would say when they made the beds together and one side of the sheet was longer than the other. If only Antonia had taken that hint as a way to deal with her overbearing mother. Or the lovely *recalculating* from her nonjudgmental GPS when Antonia takes a wrong turn, no impatience, no berating her for making a mistake. In the textbook Antonia used to use with her students, there was a whole paragraph devoted to these instances in a story: *narrative bumps* the writer puts in so the reader has to slow down and pay attention.

But Antonia's problem is that she pays *too* much attention. She's always slowing down. Reading prose as if it were poetry.

You read each word? Sam was astonished. Didn't anyone ever teach you to speed read?

What would be the point? she had challenged him back. Sometimes when he said such things, Antonia wondered if Sam and she were even of the same species. And now his spirit DNA is circulating in her system.

Closer than he appears to be, a form of immortality.

SAM! Antonia shouts his name, trying to flush him out. SAA-AM!

She swerves, pulling the wheel back just in time to avoid going over the side of the mountain.

THE AIRBNB JUST outside Athol is a sweet cuckoo-clock-type cottage with a cobblestone path leading up to the front door. Instead of a little bird, a pair of barking dogs come bounding out to greet Antonia as she gets out of the car, almost knocking her over. Mona follows, swooping down the front steps, arms out, her face a tragic mask. Oh sister, oh sister! She collapses into Antonia's arms. Another woman hangs back at a respectful distance. This must be the beautiful Maritza, or so Izzy always described her friend. A beauty, really? Broad hips and thick thighs. Her hair a boosted brown, the gray showing at the roots, her eyebrows still dark and struggling to grow in where they were once severely plucked, back in the day before Frida Kahlo or some actress playing Frida Kahlo popularized the thick brows. But maybe Maritza was a beauty once upon a time, turning the heads of men and women, with whom she was always having dramatic affairs that ended badly. Antonia recalls some story of a kidnapping, or was it a stabbing—a lover turned deadly? The beautiful Maritza, a modern-day Helen of Troy. If so, Maritza, too, has gotten older and broader. The time after the *happily ever after* of fairy tales. They all live there now.

Two more women step out of the cottage. A slender blonde, who seems to be a dog person, too, judging by how she crouches down to pet and baby-talk Maritza's pair, and a second older woman, soft and huggable, like a stuffed animal. Somebody's grandmother, with a messy bun on top of her head and funky fire-engine-red glasses speckled with tiny black stars.

Who are all these people? Antonia whispers in her sister's ear.

Izzy's posse, Mona explains, calling them over to

meet her big sister. Just saying "big sister" brings on tears. The title already transferred to the next in line.

The blonde woman introduces herself: Nancy, the Realtor. She seems unsure whether to shake hands or hug—a dilemma Antonia promptly solves by sticking out her hand. She doesn't need one more dubious friend. Nancy is tiresome with her commiserations. She is so, so sorry! Anything she can do to help, she says, handing out her cards like tissues at a funeral. I honestly had no idea. Your sister just seemed like a free spirit, super nice, generous to a fault.

All this retrospective praise is making Antonia nervous. Has her sister's body been found?

No, no, no, nothing like that, Nancy reassures her. Her aquamarine eyes glitter with moisture—but the color makes her sympathy seem phony. Nancy says she understands how worried everyone is feeling. She, too, has sisters.

The other woman is the investigator that Kempowski contracted to do some local gumshoeing, Dorothy, call her Dot. Antonia would never have guessed the elderly woman was a private investigator. But Kempowski claims Dot is the best there is in surveillance. Everyone talks to Grandma. She has been interviewing Nancy in the back sunporch. They were just finishing up. Dot will swing by Nancy's office later to pick up a copy of some signed paperwork and Izzy's cell. Nancy will hold on to Izzy's deposit for now, to be totally refunded if—

Dot and Nancy exchange a glance. No need to go there now.

Nancy leaves, tooting her horn in a way that feels too perky given the circumstances. Antonia and Mona link arms. It's the closest Antonia has felt to her baby sister in a while. They keep butting heads over how to respond to the Izzy situation.

Ay, sister, sister. Mona leans her head on Antonia's shoulder. What's that line in that poem of yours? Something about how *we make the spirit out of what we own / no angel lives abroad but in the bone.*

That is an oldie all right! Antonia laughs. I wrote that, like, in college. I don't even have a copy of it.

I don't know how many times I've quoted that poem to my patients.

Mona quoting poetry, *Antonia's* poetry no less! Did it help? Antonia wonders out loud.

I haven't a clue, Mona snorts, a rare moment of self-doubt. I mean, I think my patients felt accompanied— and that's sometimes the best we can do for each other.

If that's all we're asked to do for each other, is

Antonia off the hook by writing her poems? Or is that just outsourcing her compassion? Conveniently removing herself from the havoc that the troubled cause in the lives of others.

Mario, Estela, Izzy . . . What does she owe them? It's no longer an abstract dinner-party or classroom question. Besides, it's not for others to answer for her. *No angel lives abroad but in the bone.* The height of self-care: the divinized self. Go easy, Antonia says in her GPS voice. Recalculating . . .

INSIDE THE COTTAGE, it's like a pajama party gone awry. Maritza is giving everyone supportive back rubs. Mona uncorks a bottle of wine. Dot puts a hand over her glass. She's on the job. Just water, thanks. Dot wears no jewelry, nondescript clothing, no brands or logos. If the point is not to have any identifying marks—tabula rasa—she better get rid of those funky glasses.

Dot has run every check on Nancy—litigation and criminal history: none of the databases turned up a thing. The gal is clean. Which doesn't rule out greed, self-interest, finding an easy mark and taking aim. There is a lot in this world you can get away with and still be within your rights. It is not a crime to profit from the troubled or soon to be missing.

But what about Nancy ending up with Izzy's cell phone? Isn't that kind of fishy?

I thought the same thing. Mona nods in confirmation. But Dot has already worked this angle and lays it all out. Possession of Izzy's cell phone is not in itself suspicious. It's plausible. Say someone leaves behind their cell phone in your house. Obviously, you can't call them to let them know. You figure they'll retrace their steps once they find it missing. Remember, Nancy had no idea that Izzy was someone who had gone missing. Besides, Izzy was supposed to come back on her way home from Chicago. That's what she told Nancy. So, if worse came to worst, Nancy was planning to return the cell phone then.

Mona and Antonia lift their eyebrows at each other. An expression of incredulity all the sisters share with their mother. Mangos under the tree. They're not buying it.

I'll tell you what I would have done, Mona says with the righteousness of the aggrieved youngest whose ideas are always discounted. Mona would've gone to Recent Calls and called every last one of those numbers. Left a message. *Please let Izzy Vega know that she left her cell phone at my house.* Maritza agrees. That's what she would have done, too.

Some people are careless, Dot reminds them, giving the Realtor the benefit of the doubt. A benefit they will all need to avail themselves of in order to get out from the shadow of many doubts. Who among them hasn't been negligent toward Izzy? She wears everybody out. "You had to like burdens to love Carson," a friend of Carson McCullers was quoted in a retrospective article Antonia shared with her class. "Many of us could not afford her emotionally or economically."

The best thing we can give the people who love us is to take care of ourselves so we don't become a burden on them.

And when we do become a burden? Izzy had confronted Antonia the last time she had quoted her dictum on the phone. Izzy liked to push other people's hallowed pronouncements to outrageous conclusions. Crack open those chestnuts. Then what? she'd asked. You'll set me down on an ice floe and throw away the key? Like others in the family, Izzy was also always mixing her metaphors.

DOT WOULD LIKE to interview each sister individually. At first, Antonia suspects the private investigator of wanting to stretch out her billable time by doing separate depositions. But once she's taken into the back porch, and Dot starts plying her with questions about Mona and Tilly, Antonia understands the strategy. Digging for dirt. How did her other sisters get along with Izzy? How about Kaspar—did he sometimes clash with Izzy? And Antonia's own husband?

He's dead, Antonia says bluntly. Didn't this Dot do her due diligence? Wouldn't that come right up in an online search? Antonia Vega, 66, retired university professor, widowed. No litigation or criminal record. She did recently harbor a fugitive, set her up with an appointment at the Open Door Clinic. There is a lot in this world you can get away with and still not be found in a database.

I'm sorry to hear that, Dot says in a chastened voice. A tough time to have another loss.

My sister isn't dead yet, Antonia snaps at the other woman. They're getting off on the wrong foot. Why is she making it so difficult? What would Sam do?

Actually, Sam would probably get up and walk away. He hated when things were made more complicated than he thought they needed to be.

Dot stops her phone recorder to signal they are now off the record. I totally get how hard this is, Dot says sincerely. I'm only doing my job. All in the best interests of bringing your sister back safe and sound. But if now's not a good time . . . The sincerity laced with a veiled threat.

The cage door is open—Antonia could just fly away. But if not now, when? And she does not want to be the problematic sister. In the world according to private investigators, her prickliness would probably make her a prime suspect.

What is the right time to do things?

Let's get this over and done with.

Were there any recent blowups between Izzy and any of her sisters? Was she on medication of any kind? Was she bipolar, as sister Mona claims? There seems to have been no definitive diagnosis or treatment trail. Would Mona have any reason to malign her older sibling?

Antonia can feel the tension on her face. She recognizes her own propensity to doubt, second-guess, suspect, and judge. But Antonia does not want to live in that kind of universe, even if it turns out to be the real one. What are you getting at? she confronts Dot.

I understand your parents recently died. Was there any disagreement on the provisions of the will? Sometimes those things can tear a family apart. One sibling tries to claim more of the pot. Another sibling feels she got a raw deal.

Dot might be the best there is in gumshoeing disguised as an addled grandmother, but she has obviously not had much experience with a Latina sisterhood. Conflict is their modus operandi. Comparing, competing, bickering, issuing epithets, condescending ringtones, you name it, and at the same time, utterly loyal and bound to each other. You can't flatten that out into simple villainy.

Nor can Antonia give Dot a condensed, coherent summary of Izzy's life. It'd be like trying to contain a genie in a bottle. Several marriages, broken hearts, what Izzy has called her trail of tears. The doctoral degree that took her forever to earn. I don't know how you do it, Izzy commented to Antonia about writing her thesis. Whenever I write something, I have to leave so much out. *Not enough*, Antonia thought, as she ploughed through Izzy's thousand-page dissertation.

Then there was the period Izzy got involved in causes—never in a calm, consistent, sustainable way. Always with an element of high drama. She was going to Nicaragua to join the Sandinistas; she was going to be a human sandbag at the border; she was walking across America barefoot to call attention to the Pies Descalzos Foundation and would not put on a pair of shoes until every child in the world was shod.

But what about when it snows and you're barefoot in Kansas with half a continent to go? Antonia queried. And how will you know for sure when everyone in the world has a pair of shoes to wear?

There you go again, always ruining everyone's parade. Izzy shook her head. The naysayers she had to put up with!

Then, there was the time after the election when Izzy bought a bullhorn. She was going to park herself in front of the White House, like that lady in *The Arabian Nights* Antonia was always talking about, and tell Sultan Trump a thousand and one tales in as many nights. What do you think? she asked Antonia.

I think you'll get arrested.

Meanwhile, ordinary self-maintenance was beneath her standards. Izzy couldn't hold on to money; she fell for men who took advantage, cheated on her, stole from her, went shopping with her credit card. Lately, the rootlessness. Her house for sale, her house as refugee camp.

Even Dot is looking weary. She keeps returning to the criminal element where she's on surer ground. What about those ex-boyfriends or refugees in her house— could they have done Izzy harm?

Antonia's phone rings, a number she doesn't recognize, but she decides to take the call anyway. She needs get away from Dot's universe. She excuses herself, slips out the door of the sunporch, and walks a few steps into the dark yard to a wooden bench. Thank goodness she is sitting down when the familiar voice says, Don't get mad, okay?

SHE WAS ON her way to Tilly's. She had every intention of getting there in time for Antonia's birthday. As a matter of fact, her car is full of gifts. She just happened to be driving through a town where a pottery shop was having a liquidation—

Antonia cuts her off: Do you have any idea what we've all been through in the last—what is it now?— nine, ten days? Antonia has lost count. She is sobbing with relief. Izzy is alive! But now that she is, Antonia is ready to kill her.

Izzy does not want to be guilt-tripped. You promised you wouldn't get mad!

She did? Either way, Antonia better scale it back or Izzy is going to hang up before Antonia can get the information they need to track down their lost sister. For an unreal moment Antonia wonders if this is a trick? Izzy calling from beyond the grave. A heaven wink? A narrative bump? In which case, put Sam on!

Slowly, the rambling story sort of coheres—which is as much as can be expected of any of Izzy's narratives. Izzy was on her way to Tilly's but she had to stop to make a deposit on a motel. Turns out the people next door had llamas about to be put down, as the own-ers couldn't take care of them. Izzy offered to adopt them. Didn't you get my message? Izzy asks in a cross voice.

What message? Antonia feels she has entered an alternate universe where nothing follows logically from anything else. Why haul the llamas to Illinois? Tilly lives in the suburbs. There's probably an ordinance against llamas on Happy Valley Road.

That's why I called you, Izzy explains. They'd be bet-ter off in Vermont. I would have driven them there. But you didn't pick up.

You knew I was in Illinois, Antonia reminds Izzy. Or did this information even register with their older sister? Could Izzy also have a touch of dementia?

We could drive back from Illinois together, Izzy proposes.

If she wasn't before, Antonia is sure now. She agrees with Mona: Izzy needs help. Izzy, listen, honey, just tell me where you are, okay?

At some roadside stop, which is why she's calling. She just went into the bathroom and there was a wanted poster of her on the wall. A really bad photo. It didn't even look like her. Otherwise someone might have rec-ognized her.

Izzy, this is serious, Antonia interjects. The police are looking for you; we hired a private investigator. The time and money they've spent. Most of all, the anguish.

You're raining on my parade! Izzy scolds in her I'm-the-oldest tone of voice. How dare a younger sibling tell her what's what.

Antonia can hear it; she's losing Izzy. The only way to draw her back from the edge is to engage her in one of the sad stories that Izzy always gets involved in.

Listen, Izzy, Antonia cuts through Izzy's rant. I'm not in Illinois anymore. I'm in Athol with Mo-mo; Tilly is on her way here; we've been trying to find you. But here's the thing: I need to get back to Vermont. There's this young girl, undocumented, pregnant, about to dar a luz, alone in this world, no one else she can call on. Antonia relates the tale, heightening the pathos, not that it needs any touching up. She can feel Izzy listening. Can such empathy be a pathology?

Antonia concludes with her bargaining chip. She's not going home until Izzy is back.

I can't, Izzy wails. I signed papers. I don't have the money. And I know you guys aren't going to lend it to me. If I rob a bank, I'll end up in jail. Or in the loony bin, she jokes. So, the reality gauge is not totally off. Izzy has not lost her sense of humor. There is hope.

We can get you out of that agreement. Your Realtor friend Nancy as good as said she's ready to tear up the agreement. Antonia does not need to add the caveat: *if* something untoward has happened to the signatory. The last thing Izzy needs is an idea like that put in her head.

As she has been speaking, Antonia is walking back into the house, through the sunporch, into the living room, which has suddenly become very quiet. Mona and Maritza and Dot have sensed a surprising development. Antonia makes an emphatic gesture—jabbing a finger to her lips, then mimes writing on a piece of paper, afraid if she turns on the speakerphone, Izzy might get suspicious and hang up. Izzy, Antonia scribbles, pointing to the phone. Mona's mouth falls open, but Antonia again gestures for silence. The three women crowd around Antonia.

Ask for her location, Dot jots down.

Antonia nods deeply. Precisely what she has been trying to do. Izzy, honey, where are you, cuquita? Their mother's moniker for the favorite daughter of the moment.

Izzy again says, How should I know? Some rest stop on the interstate.

Hey! Antonia hears a male voice in the background. You're going to have to finish up. I gotta go!

Who's that? Antonia asks.

A really nice guy who is letting me use his cell. I lost mine.

Put him on, Antonia says, unsure whether Izzy will comply. Could you, please? Antonia inflects the command into a question. The eldest has to be made to feel she is in control.

Ralph sounds nice enough. Antonia explains her sister doesn't quite know where she is. Always has had a bad sense of direction—best to leave it at that in case this Ralph is some shady character for whom a vulnerable older woman, flashing her wad of cash from the bank account she emptied, would be the perfect setup.

Antonia jots down the location, Interstate 94, Exit 9, in Gary, Indiana. Dot and Mona hurry into the porch, dogs in tow, to make follow-up calls. Antonia can hear them—Dot dialing the state police; Mona, their sister Tilly. Meanwhile, Ralph really has to go. He's got a load of cream cheese to get to Chicago yesterday.

Does she offer to buy the whole truckload in exchange for Ralph babysitting Izzy before the cops come? Can you put my sister back on?

Hey! she hears Ralph shouting into the roar of interstate traffic. Your sister still wants to talk to you!

I'm afraid she just drove off, he says when he comes

back on. Don't worry. She's not going fast pulling that big trailer of animals.

IT DOESN'T TAKE long to set their rescue operation in motion. The Indiana state police have already stopped a driver swerving on the highway. Dot asks them to please hold Felicia Vega. She has been missing. The family is worried. Mona reaches Tilly and Kaspar, who were only a couple of hours away from Athol. They are turning around and racing back to Gary. Depending on what the state police might require, the plan is to pick up Izzy, and—then what? That's what the sisterhood has to decide. Where do the homeless whose ice floes have melted reside? What is the right thing to do by someone whose head isn't on right?

Another call comes in, but this time it's Beth Trotter. Just wanting to give Antonia an update. Beth has checked out the expectant mother. The position of the baby, the size of her cervix, any time now. But here's the thing. Beth has done a little of her own sleuthing. Since Estela is a minor, if she goes to the hospital without a guardian, they will have to notify DCF, who will notify ICE about an underage undocumented minor, and the likelihood is Estela will be deported before another brown US citizen can be born. It never rains but it pours, right?

Beth has already called her friend Deborah, a probate judge, who is ready to step in with an expedited guardianship. You'd be the perfect candidate, Deborah agrees. Respected professor emeritus, writer, widow of a beloved doctor, and, a biggie, you're Hispanic, able to communicate with the girl pending her special juvenile status hearing. But we're racing against the clock here. How soon before you'll be back?

Who is the most important one? Antonia could torture herself. But the answer is plain as day. They now know where Izzy is. The state police already have her in custody. Tilly is turning around on the interstate. They're in for the long haul now, getting Izzy into treatment, monitoring her meds, a residential facility perhaps. In the meantime—

Oh my God! Beth exclaims when Antonia explains her situation. Sorry to have dumped all this on you right now. You've got enough on your plate. It never rains but it pours all right.

Antonia is soaking wet. On the narrow path. Every self-help podcast advises her to take care of herself first. But the objects in the mirror come closer.

EIGHT

All it takes

Back home, Antonia's answering machine is blinking. A dozen or so hang ups. Finally, one of the messages has content: Toni, are you there? Please pick up! Hello! I know you're there! Izzy's voice is urgent. She's pretending she's not there, Izzy complains to someone at her end. The line goes dead.

Tuesday, 5:30 p.m., the machine voice announces. A day ago. Izzy must have called the landline before reaching Antonia on her cell number in Athol.

The next message is again Izzy. Sorry, she didn't mean to hang up. She's using somebody else's cell. She lost hers. I really need to reach you, she pleads. I have a *huuuuuge* favor to ask.

Can Toni—oops, sorry, can Antonia take in some homeless llamas that are otherwise going to end up as dogmeat? Izzy was going to buy a farm but she doesn't think she can swing it right now. You've got a ton of land around your house, Izzy pleads. It's a family, the mom and dad, and the cutest little baby. All it would take is fencing in a little area and building a small shed for them to get in out of the weather in winter.

All it would take . . . A little of this, a little of that, the English version of Izzy's beloved -itos in Spanish.

I'll pay for it with my own money, Izzy adds, her stock phrase when she does not want to abide by majority rule. A few years back it was decisions around their parents' care. Izzy wanted her sisters to pitch in and buy their mother eighty-three orchid plants for her eighty-third birthday. The sisters declined. Mami was already so forgetful with her Alzheimer's. How was she to take care of them? And where on earth would she put eighty-three orchids in the cramped apartment?

In the yard, of course! Izzy replied, with a tone of What do you take me for? A dummy?

But Izzy knew very well that Mami never went down to the yard anymore. The stairs were too steep.

So, we put in one of those electric chair elevators. They have seatbelts, you know?

Izzy, honey, don't you hear how crazy this sounds? Antonia tried to reason. So did Tilly and Mona when Izzy called them up to complain about *your sister Antonia, always raining on our parades.* For once, the three hung together, united against Izzy's wild schemes.

Never mind then! Izzy would go ahead and get Mami her birthday orchids with her own money and sign the card from *your four daughters,* shaming them into complying.

Antonia had to wonder: what *own money* did Izzy have left by now for rescuing llamas, no less buying a motel or a farm? How much did she get on the sale of her house? Has it even closed yet? Antonia was surprised to learn that Izzy had as much as ten grand in an account. Last time she and Sam had invited Izzy for a visit—was it only last March for Antonia's sixty-fifth birthday? A stab of pain, remembering how much can happen in a year!—her sister's excuse was she didn't have any money for gas.

At the time, Izzy was still living in Boston in her house. You don't even need a full tank to get here, Antonia pointed out. I'll pay for your gas with my own money, Antonia added, not without irony, the unkind kind.

On her call yesterday, Izzy had lamented that she didn't have any money left to finish paying for the motel.

So how can she afford maintaining a family of llamas? But Izzy has never been one to be bothered with such practical details. Besides, she had moved on to the bad photo on her wanted poster at the rest stop bathroom. Izzy, pobrecita, with her runaway mind. No root system for that larger-than-life spirit. There must be an opera, maybe a modern one, about someone like her.

Antonia is about to erase Izzy's rambling messages, but she decides to keep them. In case the sisters have to prove to some judge that their sister needs their guardianship to help her navigate her way between the Scylla and Charybdis of her manic highs and depressive lows.

Does anyone know what I'm referring to? Antonia had asked her students, noting their baffled looks when she mentioned Scylla and Charybdis. Another way she marked the passing of her generation, their expressions, tastes, habits—eye-rollingly passé to these new arrivals in the field of time. Like, is it a movie about two rogue women taking off together? one girl surmised with that questioning uplift of the female voice, answering a question with a question.

She's thinking of *Thelma & Louise*, I think, a classmate offered, turning a puzzled look at Professor Vega. Weren't they, like, dragons or monsters?

Antonia loved those moments when her students

betrayed a childlike wonder and curiosity in learning the names of things. *Heaven lies about us in our infancy! / Shades of the prison-house begin to close / Upon the growing boy.* But there are those who never get to enjoy that heaven even in infancy, she would tell her students now. The default for most of the world is not happiness. Why then do we feel aggrieved when suffering strikes us? Who can Antonia ask?

THE LAST MESSAGE is from Sheriff Boyer. He clears his throat when the beep sounds and he's suddenly on the spot. Just checking in that, hmm, that everything's okay. He's driven by the house several times and the place looked awful quiet. He'll swing by on his way home. Time of his call three thirty this very afternoon. It's closing on six now. Antonia better call him right away and cut him off at the pass before he shows up.

His card is under the UNCLE SAM WANTS YOU magnet on her refrigerator, the "Uncle" crossed out—one of the many magnets sent by her sisters over the years and one of the few she has kept. Antonia scrapped the majority of them. After Sam's death, their banalities irritated her. She'd slam the fridge door so hard, the wise words fell to the floor. LIFE IS WHAT HAPPENS WHILE WE ARE MAKING OTHER PLANS. DON'T LET YESTERDAY

TAKE UP TOO MUCH OF TODAY. YOU DON'T HAVE TO BE PERFECT TO BE AMAZING. IF YOU'RE GOING THROUGH HELL, KEEP GOING. (That one she has kept as well.) The sheriff picks up on the second ring. Well, howdy—

She got his message, just got in herself, been away, a bunch of other calls to make, thanks so much for checking in.

Glad everything's okay, just thought he'd drop over on his way to the Mexican place.

The Mexican place? He must mean Lulu's. One of the undocumented migrant mothers, an enterprising older women, Lulu began by making meals for the growing migrant population homesick for home cooking. The wife on the farm where Lulu was living with her son approached her about starting a business together. The wife would front the operation. After a few months they had to rent space—a small house on the way to the town dump that used to be a florist shop, then a beauty salon; now it's the Mexican place with no shingle out front for obvious reasons. It's all word of mouth, which is why it's unsettling that the sheriff knows about it. They do a lot of takeout, home deliveries to different farms. Lulu's son even built a stand on wheels, which the farm wife and her daughter haul out to the parking lot at Shaw's at lunch. It's like a big open secret: the county

is flooded with undocumented workers doing everything from milking to cooking tasty lunches: enchiladas,
tacos, chili con carne, refried beans, you say how hot
you want them.

Love her cooking, the sheriff smacks his lips to prove
it. Hey, can he interest Antonia in some takeout this
evening?

Could the man be serious? It's not yet a year after losing Sam. When is the right time to ask a widow on a date?
But even if it had been years, let's face it, she has zero
interest in Sheriff Boyer. Why postpone a permanent no?

Because in Izzy's universe and Sam's, the universe
Antonia wants to live in, there's always room for one
more. And maybe Sheriff Boyer's just being a good
neighbor. Or maybe the man himself is needing to find
something or someone to help him plug the hole in his
own heart? He is in his late fifties, she guesses, living
with his mother, divorced, perhaps with scattered or
estranged children.

Antonia hesitates, a hair's-breadth pause that always
gets her in trouble—it used to with Sam, now with
Mario, Estela, always with Izzy. Maybe some other time,
Antonia says, her voice lifting like her female students. I
just got back, a bunch of calls . . .

Okay then, no takeout tonight. But he'd still like to

swing by. Something he needs to talk to her about. Of a personal nature.

Antonia's skin prickles. She has developed an allergy to surprises of a personal nature. Any hint what it's about?

It should take up only a few minutes of your time, he answers with a nonanswer.

A few minutes of her time. All it would take. Three llamas. Eighty-three orchids. In a matter of months, Mami's orchids had died in their hanging gourd planters from overwatering or neglect. An omen, Izzy pronounced, heartbroken, that Mami would die before her eighty-third year was over. And that time, Izzy had been right.

WHILE ANTONIA AWAITS the sheriff, she puts in a call next door. Mario, how are things?

Bien.

¿Y Estela? ¿Cómo está? ¿Bien?

Sí.

Curt, one-word answers. The *doñitas* have gone out of his voice. The same frustrating generic summaries that Sam would always give her instead of newsy reports. As for putting on Estela, she's not there, next door cleaning for el patrón. With that huge belly, days from giving birth? Better not chide the disgruntled boyfriend and get on his bad side. Antonia is still hoping for a lovers' reconciliation. Too many years of teaching *Pride and Prejudice* and *Romeo and Juliet*. It gets in your blood.

Can you tell her I called? An abrupt *sí*. Antonia wonders if Mario will convey the message at all. She better look in on Estela herself after the sheriff's visit.

She also needs to call Beth Trotter and let her know. On the drive home from Athol, Antonia had a lot of "recalculating" time. With whatever long process Izzy's care will involve, Antonia is going to have to recuse herself from taking in a minor with a baby and no papers. She cannot abide in the wide open spaces her sister inhabits. Antonia had hoped that with time she could shed those smaller selves—what therapy was supposed to help with, so she thought. Instead, it looks like she's going to have to learn to live with the disappointment of not being as grand as she would like to be. *If I try to be like you, who will be like me?* her former therapist had quoted every time Antonia got down on herself, one of a repertoire of Yiddish sayings her therapist's grandmother had quoted to her as a child. There was also one about Abraham at Heaven's gate, but that one is foggier in Antonia's mind. She always messes up God's punch line.

* * *

SHERIFF BOYER IS in obvious discomfort. Instead of touching his hat in salute, he takes it off, a cue that he wants to be asked in.

Come in, Antonia says, already cautioning herself not to invite him as far as her living room. A few minutes of her time, that's all he's going to get.

Sorry to bother you, he mutters, looking at his feet. That spot where inchoate males often look to for coaching on what to say. For a big man with a gun in a holster and a star on his chest to be so tied up in knots is surprising and somehow endearing.

Antonia has no inkling what he wants—rare when other people's lines aren't already projected in her head. Surprising? Refreshing, actually.

Sheriff Boyer wants her to know, he says, giving her a quick glance before he goes back to reading his lines from his boots, that he has the greatest respect for Mexicans. You all know how to work; that's a fact.

She's not Mexican, but never mind. She's not about to set him straight. He's having a hard enough time.

You all are doing the jobs no one else wants to do. Matter of fact, his family's dairy farm went under some years back. His father couldn't make a go of it. Had he had a couple of these boys, the Boyer family would still own those hundred acres over on Snake Mountain Road where that development is now. He's gone off script, no longer staring at his shoes.

And your point being . . . ? Antonia used to prompt her rambling students.

Take that Lulu. The sheriff shakes his head in wonder. You ever taste one of her chicken empanadas?

Antonia pulls her gaze away from the stout man's belly, protruding over his belt buckle. She decides not to tell him she's vegetarian. Lulu's a good cook, she agrees.

Good doesn't begin to touch it. A woman like that's worth her weight in gold.

Lulu is built solid. Cast in gold, she'd be worth a ton. But then, another thought replaces the image of Lulu as a golden block. Antonia had wondered whether the sheriff was hitting on her, but maybe Boyer is taken not only by the chicken empanadas but by the attractive Mexican woman who cooks them.

In my line of work—the sheriff's voice has thickened— we get insider information all the time. We don't get involved in immigration enforcement. Someone doesn't break the law, it's of no concern of ours. But we hear things, is the point. Sheriff Boyer happens to have heard that the folks up in St. Albans are planning a raid down this way. Just saying. In his line of work. He hears things.

One phone call to Mario or José, and in a matter of

minutes, every undocumented farm worker in the county will be alerted. How soon? Antonia asks the sheriff.

They're working on some federal order to be sure all their i's are dotted and t's crossed. Maybe as soon as this weekend? he offers, answering her question with a question—apparently, it's not the purview of females only. I figured, you knowing Spanish, you could maybe spread the word? And maybe also let Lulu know? Best not do it by phone as those calls can be tracked. And he'd appreciate it if Antonia doesn't mention her source. We don't get involved, you understand.

Antonia nods. Sure, she'll alert folks. It's not a crime to be a gossip, is it? But the bigger issue is the answer to the question she now poses to the sheriff: What do you advise people do? People. Every noun divested of identifying adjectives. No brand names. She thinks of Dot. What would Grandma say?

If I were them—a big leap of the imagination, which he takes—I'd make myself scarce. Not be out on the road, delivering tacos, or wiring money at Shaw's. For right now, anyhow. I'm real sorry about all this, he concludes.

Turns out they do have this being sorry in common. Antonia thanks him at the door. It was big of you to let me know.

Know what? he asks, grinning as he wipes his finger-prints from the kind deed he has done.

As she watches the sheriff drive away, Antonia wonders what has gotten into the man, putting himself out this way. Might not be that he's taken with Lulu. Why does her mind instantly run to that default romantic plot? It no longer applies to her, for one. Could it be something as simple as kindness? Or love? The agape kind, not eros, a distinction she often pointed out to her students, who slathered the word *love* on every boy/girl heartache. Embodied in a man who could so easily fall into the stereotype that Antonia and her friends often banish the Jesus folks, the political right-wingers, the gunslingers and xenophobes. Her own othering of others. Whatever is driving him, Sheriff Boyer's not going to turn the tide of meanness sweeping over the country, but at least he's saved a handful of "her" people from being carried away.

ESTELA RUNS INTO the mudroom when she hears Antonia's voice at Roger's door. Doñita, doñita. Antonia's heart floods with warmth at the girl's undisguised joy, reminding her of those times when babies reach out their hands to her. Is this what mothers feel toward their children?

Estela is full of excitement. El patrón is letting her earn a little money helping inside the house. You'd think she'd gotten a fancy job in a high-rise office with a picture window of Lake Champlain. It occurs to Antonia that this might be Estela's first paying job.

The mudroom connects into the kitchen, which seems to host every activity in addition to cooking. The air smells savory, a carnita Estela has fried up for el patrón to have for his cena. So, you know how to cook? Antonia asks foolishly before she thinks through that Estela has probably never had the luxury of someone else making her meals, no less choosing among the menu options offered in the college's dining halls. On faculty-student supper nights, Antonia was astonished by the variety. She had read that colleges had upped the ante of perks in competing for students: a food court of offers, condominium living, stables for their horses. Or llamas, probably. *If you don't see it, ask!* said the sign by one of the food stations.

Estela laughs. Of course, she knows how to cook, and she just learned how to do a laundry americano. She pats the washer and dryer in the entryway to the kitchen—máquinas that do her work for her and she still gets paid. Giggles of mischievous delight. There's a television on one counter and beside it a boom box, which Antonia has also heard blaring in the barn—portable entertainment for Roger during long milking hours. Every surface seems to be piled high with catalogs, pieces of equipment, old newspapers. Tacked on the wall is a cartoonish sketch of a leering tractor—that's what it looks like, the top part of an old calendar Champlain Valley Equipment gives out every year, the bottom pages with the months torn off. Roger probably thought the sketch amusing and saved it. Like opera, farm art is an acquired taste. There she goes again, shoving someone down her othering chute.

Estela smiles proudly, as Antonia surveys the girl's handiwork. A shining path has been mopped from the doorway to the stove. The curtains look freshly washed and ironed. There's a stack of clean dishes and gleaming water glasses on the cramped counter. Estela was just finishing up with the last of the pots and pans.

Antonia pulls away to get a full-length look at the pregnant girl. She nods at the enormous belly. Should Estela be doing all this housework?

Estela giggles again. Ay, doñita! Mi mamá, mis tías, primas—all of them worked until they gave birth, then rested a few hours, before going back to their oficios. That's the way it's done, Estela says with an assurance that might soon be tested in another kind of labor—without her mother, tías, older cousins around to fortify her with their certainties as she gives birth. One of the many losses accompanying the major loss of a homeland. Just as with Sam: Antonia is constantly ambushed by some painful reminder of his absence: his empty napkin ring in a drawer, the duct-tape repair he performed on the old vacuum cleaner, his boot jack in the back of the coat closet.

La doctora was very nice, Estela reports. She says everything looks good. El bebé is healthy and strong. La doctora wants Estela to take lessons. As far as Antonia can tell, it's a free natural childbirth class sponsored by the hospital. But Estela cannot go because she has no *rrride*. It takes Antonia a moment to realize that Estela is using the English word, but mispronouncing it like a Spanish word. Less than a couple of weeks here and already speaking Spanglish.

Antonia broaches the delicate subject of Mario. Estela hesitates, but before she can speak up, Roger enters the room from outdoors.

Sorry to barge in, Antonia greets him. We were just catching up.

Be my guest, Roger says. Maybe the tasty meal that awaits him has opened up not just his appetite but his heart.

So, tell me, ¿cómo va todo? Antonia returns to the

troublesome question. Estela again glances toward Roger, washing his hands at the sink. Acuérdate: el señor no entiende español, Antonia reminds the girl. Estela can tell her the truth in Spanish without any risk of Roger understanding.

Estela confesses that Mario still wants nothing to do with her. She seems on the verge of tears, so Antonia drops the subject and asks Roger if she can have a word with him. Not a good idea to speak of the coming raid with Estela in the room. The girl might not understand the content but she'll pick up on the tension. She has already been through more than enough. *Sufficient unto the day is the evil thereof.* Why hasn't anyone made that into a magnet? Another demographic's chestnut. Maybe it's time to reinstate it in her circles?

Out in the mudroom, Roger stamps his foot when Antonia alerts him about the immigration enforcement plans. Goddamn damn it all! Interfering government people. What's he supposed to do? He glares at Antonia as if it's her doing, this Scylla-Charybdis predicament he is in. Another modern equivalent she might have mentioned to her students, citing her neighbor's no-win situation, either break the law or lose his farm.

I asked my source the same thing, Antonia explains. I was told the best thing is to keep the workers on the farm. No driving them into town for groceries or other errands.

Roger jerks his head toward the kitchen, where they can hear the sounds of Estela finishing up her cleaning. What about her? I can't be responsible for driving her to the hospital when her time comes.

As soon as Izzy is in their custody, Antonia will have to leave town again. Who knows what the next few months will entail, connecting Izzy with the treatment she needs. Tilly will head back to Ill-y-noise, and Mona to North Carolina. As the close-by sister, Antonia will have her hands full. More than enough good excuses to pass on Estela's care. Antonia has got to stand firm. But still, it feels wrong to be playing hot potato with a human being.

I can take her for a couple of nights until I have to leave again, Antonia offers. Maybe she can ask Lulu, who knows everyone in the migrant community, for any suggestions. Maybe Lulu can house the forlorn girl and her baby. Estela could even help out with the cooking, earn a little money herself. Of course, Lulu will soon be scrambling to close up her kitchen, sounding the alarm among the migrant workers in the county. The migra is coming, the migra is coming. Antonia can feel the agitation in her own heart. It's going to be a job keeping everyone from panicking.

Antonia recalls how patients would often call Sam in the middle of the night full of dread over some pain or problem. He always managed to calm them. What is it he would do that she can do now? Once she had asked him how he navigated his way past the Scylla and Charybdis moments in his life? (She had already explained the allusion, years back.) He thought it over, then shook his head. All he could think of was what his mother would always say when she found herself in a tough situation, drying her hands on her apron, Well, let's see what love can do.

Another fridge magnet: this one with Sam's mom's words. But Sam would scoff at needing to highlight what was only common sense and basic decency. Be like reminding yourself to breathe—which Antonia reminded him has been a reminder given to her by any number of yoga and meditation teachers over the years. Let's see what love can do, Antonia counsels herself now. The answers won't come easy or quick or maybe at all. Maybe just asking the question will calm her enough to continue through the confusion of the present moment to whatever small certitude awaits.

While Estela collects her things in a satchel at the trailer, Antonia delivers the news to José and Mario. They are grim and silent. What will el patrón do now?

The two men look to her, as if she were their puppeteer. ¿Nos vamos? Do they run before they are thrown out—of the farm and the country?

Right now, the best move is to stay calm, not leave the farm for any reason. She's taking Estela with her por si acaso. In case the girl goes into labor tonight. Antonia will drive her to the hospital. It's all I've told her, Antonia says, lowering her voice. Best not to worry her with this troubling information for now.

But what if you are stopped? Mario wants to know. What will they do with Estela? Will she be deported? A good sign, Antonia thinks, his showing some curiosity if not yet full-blown concern about the girl he has discarded.

We will be fine, she assures him. It's unlikely the sheriff would stop her to inquire about the pregnant girl riding beside her. In fact, Boyer might even give her a police escort, lights flashing, to the ER if Antonia were to ask. He's probably in his kitchen now eating his chicken empanadas with his mother, not knowing—or perhaps knowing—what panic will soon be traveling through the bloodstream of the underground population in his county. To his credit, Boyer did what love would allow him to do given his position as sheriff at this moment in time. Maybe there will be more to do and he will do it.

ON THE DRIVE back to the house, Estela chatters about all the new things she has discovered in the last few days since Antonia left. El patrón's televisor, his popcorn machine, a lámpara that swirls with a thick gelatinous substance. Roger has a lava lamp! The magical theme park that is the First World to the migrant, the refugee, the wretched refuse from other teeming shores, until the discovery that admission to the magic show is denied them.

Suddenly, a conejo jumps into the headlights. Antonia veers and misses. *Rabbit*. Estela recalls the word in English from Antonia's lessons during their drive a few days ago. Several more words come as they pass familiar landmarks out the window.

You are a very good student, Antonia praises her.

I finished la primaria, Estela brags. Until her mother needed her at home. Six little sisters to help take care of. A small plot of land to farm.

¿Y estrella? Antonia points at a star in the darkening sky, testing her stellar student. But Estela can't recall the word in English. Star, Antonia pronounces. Same as your name. *Estela* means *star*, you know?

Estar, Estela repeats, mispronouncing the English so that it sounds like *estar* in Spanish. Antonia recalls the little rhyme she was taught to distinguish between *ser* for permanence and *estar* for what is flecting. *For how you feel or where you are, always use the verb estar.*

Estar, estar, Estela practices, giggling each time she is corrected. As they turn into the drive, the floodlights come on, the garage door lifts. Estela claps her hands in wonder and delight. The world of el norte is indeed magical.

Doñita, why can't I live here, too? If my child is born here, he will have the right, and I, his mother, won't? The great injustice of circumstance, Antonia might say to a class of her students. What to say to this girl? *We will see what love can do?*

NINE

Air quotes

Good news! the sisters report. Izzy has now been reunited with Tilly and Mona. They have set up an intervention in Boston with a psychiatrist who is the leading light on bipolar disorders. It would be ideal if all three sisters were present. Just saying, Mona says, when Antonia protests that it sounds like overkill. Izzy will feel ganged up on. Two sisters should be more than enough.

United, we stand, divided, Izzy falls, Mona counters.

This is good news? Antonia wonders. The new normal. The new good news. Shouldn't the phrase be in air quotes? Is there a way to air quote when no one can see your hands? A tone of voice. *He-llo-oh?!* her students would say, in a singsong, to suggest irony.

The appointment is a day away, Friday. How soon can Antonia get here?

Let me see what I can do, Antonia gives in.

After calling around to her contacts in the migrant community—no one is available now that the alert is out—Antonia decides to ask Beth Trotter. Would she mind keeping Estela for a few days while Antonia attends to a family emergency?

Beth hesitates. I suppose I can put her in the twins' room. It's warm enough; they can sleep in the screened-in porch. Do you know what she likes to eat? We're not big on Mexican food over here, but I hear there's a stand in the parking lot at Shaw's where all the nurses go for lunch.

It's so much easier when someone just says no, n-o, as Roger has no trouble doing, instead of dragging you through all their considerations. Antonia feels disappointed, not exactly in Beth Trotter, but in the oft-failed experiment of being humane human beings. More generously, Antonia reminds herself that Beth Trotter does work full time at the hospital's OB-GYN practice and still finds time to volunteer at the Open Door Clinic.

She's also a single mom with two teenage daughters. (Officer Morgan on the night shift with nicks on his face comes to mind.) Everyone has a story. Sometimes in asking for the best of each other, it's best not to know it.

And Antonia would feel the same way if someone parked their worthy cause at her door. In fact, someone did, knocked, and then vanished. I can try someone else, Antonia offers.

No, no! Just thinking out loud. Of course she can stay here, Beth Trotter insists. How can I say no to an old friend?

Actually, it was Sam who was her colleague on the staff of the hospital. In fact, Sam was on the search committee that brought Beth here. Is there an expiration date on the tendrils of a gratitude after the mother root expires?

I really appreciate it, Beth. I know it's a lot to ask.

Are you kidding? Beth says generously. The least I can do. Did I tell you about the time that Sam spelled me when Emily had her ski accident?

Antonia has heard the story a number of times before. But she owes it to Beth to listen. In their small town, it seems everyone wants to tell Antonia their Sam story. A testament to how much he was respected and loved. These narratives are a kind of offering—to what god Antonia cannot guess. All she knows is that for the moment she is its reluctant priestess.

MONA AND TILLY have booked side-by-side rooms at the Comfort Inn an hour out of Boston: Tilly and Kaspar in one, and Mona and Izzy in the suite, which has a pullout couch in the living area where Antonia can sleep. It's only for a couple of nights, Mona points out crossly when Antonia at first insists on getting her own room. This isn't childhood. Get over it.

Tomorrow morning the sisters are meeting with the psychiatrist; the hope is that Izzy will consent to go into residential care, where she can be evaluated and her medications monitored. Afterward, the three sisters will have to come up with a long-term plan for managing Izzy's illness. Her bills will need to be paid as well as other expenses incurred in hunting her down and procuring this sort of happy ending. Realtor Nancy has convinced the motel owners to tear up Izzy's purchase agreement. Everything under control, as their mother's caretaker used to say when the sisters would call in for a daily report.

Izzy has retreated to the suite bedroom with one of her migraines, no doubt brought on by the fact that she is furious at her sisters for engineering this intervention.

Not to mention, which she does, often, having the state police hold her like a common criminal. The room is dark, the shades drawn, when Antonia enters, announcing that she wants a big hug. Start with the positive.

Go fuck yourself, Izzy greets her back. This is more Tilly's foul mouth talk than Izzy's, whose frustrations tend more toward those air quotes and a lot of *yadda yadda yaddas* for stuff she doesn't want to go into.

You're all allowed to have your lives, but I'm not allowed to have mine. Like you're all so competent and healthy. Izzy launches into her laundry list of the destructive, hypocritical behaviors of each sister: booze, cigarettes, weed, workaholism, greed, and the most recent, animal cruelty. Oh, yes! Mo-mo, the big dog lover and animal rights activist, called a shelter. The llamas have been taken away to who knows what grim fate. You're all a bunch of narcissists. The problem with having sisters who are therapists, Antonia has often noted, is that you get all kinds of diagnoses thrown at you that you can't defend yourself against.

We *are* awful. You're absolutely right, Antonia responds, some long-ago buried instruction resurfacing to always agree with the mad and the furious. She is perched at the edge of Izzy's bed after a sobbing reunion—on her part, that is; dry-eyed Izzy sits by, observing her with narrowed eyes. Antonia, too, has betrayed her, by joining this plot against her happiness.

On the other side of the closed door, Mona is speaking on the phone, updating the psychiatrist contact. Their sister is still refusing to cooperate. It seems the next step will have to be contacting a lawyer to issue an emergency guardianship order so the sisters can proceed in getting Izzy the help she needs. They have plenty of evidence of her craziness. Antonia is not sure she will volunteer the messages left on her answering machine. Of course she wants to help Izzy, but she is feeling a familiar discomfort at being in a majority against the lone holdout; so often in their family, that holdout has been she.

Antonia tries to reason with her sister. All you have to do is meet with this woman. A version of Izzy's *All it would take*.

I'm not meeting with her! I'm not fucking bipolar!

Antonia decides to back off before Izzy goes into another of her rants. Hell has no fury like the eldest being subordinated by younger siblings she is used to bossing around. Ya, ya, she soothes Izzy. *Let's see what love can do*, she soothes herself.

She strokes Izzy's thin arms—a body she knows well from having one so similar. They are the two sisters who look the most alike. In childhood photos, it's hard to distinguish between them. It didn't help that their mother—the soul of efficiency—dressed them in identical outfits in different colors—Izzy's, yellow, and Antonia's, pink, a cliché girlie-girl color Antonia rejected in her rebellious adolescent years, though as a child she had gloated over having gotten the best color. Her crowing, though, woke up no envy in Izzy. Yellow was the absolute best all-around color, the color of the sun, without which, where would the earth be? In their hippie teens, she couldn't resist pointing out to Antonia: Why do you think the Beatles chose a yellow submarine? Even now, in her sixties, Antonia doesn't own a single piece of yellow clothing. Her big sister might come charging into the Town Hall Theatre or grocery store and rip off her yellow scarf or jacket, crying out, Thief! It'd be right up Izzy's alley—making a scene.

What most moves her now is the birthmark airplane on Izzy's left wrist. It seems like a lifetime since Antonia last saw it. An omen, Izzy had reported one of her many santera guides had told her. Was Izzy's pursuit of santeras, her belief in omens and portents, going way back to when they were kids, were all of these proclivities already signs of a mental disorder? Antonia knows what her sister would say to that. Izzy once led the charge in her profession on the First World tendency of psychologists to pathologize the emotive and belief systems of countries and cultures like their own DR, demeaning them with terms such as *underdeveloped, Third World, impoverished*. Instead of the old conquistadors and missionaries, the rescuers are now well-meaning NGOs, Peace Corps volunteers, and development workers who come in with aid and answers. Another kind of conquest. Izzy can be razor-sharp in her dissections of systemic injustice, corporate greed, B.S. in general. There was a time, Antonia recalls, when Izzy was a hotshot in the field, invited to lecture to medical students at Harvard on culturally sensitive and respectful treatment of their "Third World patients." Izzy would jab the air with her air quotes.

Izzy's face suddenly softens. Gone is the wild look of the manic sister. How's your little friend? she asks, her voice as composed as if all the drama has been just that, a production in which she had to play her part.

What little friend?

Izzy closes her eyes and expels a breath—the world disappointing her again. How can her own sister not know immediately what she, Izzy, is thinking? It's a great effrontery to discover other people aren't you. Here we go again, Antonia can't help noticing: the same issue as with Sam. God made only one mistake, she'd challenge him. He didn't make me you! That shut him right up. Ha! Finally, she got the last word.

The girl you told me about, Izzy reminds Antonia. She was about to have a baby.

Even in her worst crisis, Izzy has these moments when her heart opens and makes room for someone else. If only Antonia could hold her there "forever," to borrow Izzy's air quotes.

Antonia recounts the latest Estela news, including the sheriff's visit, the imminent raid.

So where is she now?

One of Sam's colleagues took her in for a few days while I'm down here. The boyfriend won't have anything to do with her. And, no, Antonia has no idea what will become of the girl and her baby. She, Antonia, certainly can't take this on right now.

She can almost hear her words landing on the soft ground of her sister's heart. What, as young women, they used to call "the real me." The Buddha in me bowing to the Buddha in you.

I'll take her in, Izzy offers, pushing aside the covers and sitting up. It's the most energized she has been since the conversation started. The llamas. The eighty-three orchids. The migrant artist revolution. The motel to house them. The farm to feed them. Now the pregnant teenager and the fatherless child she will soon give birth to.

Ay, Izzy, Antonia sighs, moved in spite of her exasperation. You have to start by taking care of yourself. The mantra of the First World. First, your own oxygen mask, then everyone else's.

Izzy lets herself fall back on the bed. What for?

What do you mean "what for"?

All this goddamn self-care? "What's it all about, Alfie?" her sister sings, a favorite song of their teen years.

"Is it just for the moment we live?" Antonia sings back, trying to brush off the question. Sometimes it's not the right time to address the existential angle. One day at a time. One foot in front of the other—that's the road she's traveling and wants to encourage Izzy to travel.

How's the migraine, by the way? Antonia changes the subject, something that never works with any of the sisters or ever worked with their mother. Dogs with a bone—all four. Just like Mami. The mango tree, the mangoes.

Forget it, Izzy says, rolling over, turning her back to Antonia. Leave me alone, she says, shrugging Antonia's hand from her shoulder. If you're not going to help me, at least help that poor kid.

Antonia feels a flash of anger. Everyone is always telling her what she should do! Starting with Sam, who claimed it was because Antonia didn't know her own mind. Into the vacuum of her considerations he would step with his big, clunky certainties. She's suddenly angry at him, too.

If he were alive, this would be the moment when they'd have one of their fights. That, too, is over. Which makes her all the angrier. Again, and once and for all, he has the last word.

Dr. Campbell has an appealing, androgynous look, with the toned forearms of someone who works out, a firm handshake, no makeup, no wiles or easy smiles. The only whimsy is a purple strand in her brown spiked hair, signaling something, Antonia is not sure what. Her students would know. Who will teach her these things anymore?

Dr. Campbell escorts the sisters into her office, lined with shelves stocked with what look to be textbooks, the flank of volumes punctuated here and there by a snow globe or paperweight. No family photos. Perhaps, as with PI Dot, that personal a touch would give too much away.

Dr. Campbell greets Izzy as Dr. Vega, a courtesy that will endear her to Izzy, who—as she likes to remind her

sisters when they get uppity with what they know—did
earn a doctorate in psychology. And not a half-assed
MSW or one of those "honorary" doctorates like the
ones they've given to Antonia for being a blabbermouth
author, spilling everyone's beans in the family and calling it fiction, but a real bona fide sheepskin that took her
a decade to earn, with the help of Antonia's edits and
a hypnotist to boost her confidence. (So had it already
started then, the paralyzed will, the lack of confidence,
the tiny chemical worm in her brain?)

May I call you Felicia? Dr. Campbell asks Izzy, who
makes a face. Call me Izzy, as in, dizzy Izzy, she says, glar-
ing at her sisters. She's heard their "secret" epithet for her.

Izzy? Dr. Campbell smiles tentatively. Please call me
Kim.

It's unsettling to entrust a beloved sister's psyche to
someone named Kim. Dr. Campbell, Antonia persists in
calling her.

Dr. Campbell has a calm, focused manner. The old
iron hand in a velvet glove. She must be in her early
forties. *She could be my daughter*, Antonia muses, as
she often used to with her students—first, thinking
they could be her kids, then, by the time she retired,
her grandkids. Dr. Campbell wants to hear from Izzy
what she is experiencing. Let your sister explain, please,

she admonishes whenever the other sisters interrupt to correct Izzy's version of the story of the last couple of weeks. Back in childhood, when Mami was the referee, such preferential treatment would have brought on jealous accusations. You're playing favorites! That's not fair! But Antonia guesses Dr. Campbell's approach is a therapeutic strategy, not favoritism.

According to Izzy, her sisters totally overreacted. She was headed to Tilly's house, but then one thing led to another, including losing her cell so she couldn't very well call and inform them she had changed her plans. Right? Absolutely, Dr. Campbell nods, as if this is indeed reasonable. She is no fool, though, nudging gently. What about some llamas I heard you picked up? And did you say you had put some money down on a motel?

To hear Izzy's version, she acted with total moral and emotional probity. And she believes it, too. But then Antonia's never known Izzy to lie in order to deceive or mislead. It's more that she lies to make things more like they ought to be.

What's wrong with that? Izzy has challenged Antonia. How's it any different from you and your fiction? Izzy holds no one's cow sacrosanct.

The process continues and is so circuitous, Antonia wonders if Dr. Campbell will ever get to the point, make a diagnosis, and get Izzy into treatment. Or is "Kim" getting snowed by Izzy, the consummate con artist, charming, smart? The wild and wooly sister, everyone's favorite in the sitcom version of their lives.

How about we try this, just to be sure? Dr. Campbell finally suggests in the velvety voice of hidden steel. To assuage her sisters' concerns but also to follow up on Izzy's own complaints of migraines and seizures, problems that could result in mini strokes, memory loss, or worse, wouldn't it be a good idea to have Izzy check herself in for a thorough evaluation?

Dr. Campbell has just uttered the hot-button phrase, *memory loss*. Dementia has to be Izzy's biggest dragon, given their mother's demise from Alzheimer's.

Any number of physiological factors could be contributing to Izzy's symptoms, Dr. Campbell elaborates. That's why she is recommending a minimum of two weeks of testing and evaluation. Consider it a kind of a spa for your soul, Dr. Campbell adds with a lusty laugh. Wouldn't we all love to have that kind of time-out for our souls? Dr. Campbell turns to Izzy's sisters, who all nod like obedient dashboard dogs with springs in their necks.

Izzy seems to be considering the doctor's proposal. She herself has been thinking about having some tests done, she confesses. Did Kim know that their mother had Alzheimer's? And does the doctor know about the study done by researchers at Columbia Presbyterian that found that Dominicans have a genetic propensity because of all their intermarriages? That's what you get for only marrying your white cousins. Or pretend white cousins. We all have black behind the ears, Izzy quotes the Dominican saying. There follows a long tangent into the slave trade, their dark-skinned tíos and tías claiming suntans, Izzy and Antonia's tight, verging-on-kinky hair.

Dr. Campbell listens patiently. All the more reason this testing might actually be valuable to the whole family.

Izzy states her terms: she wants her evaluation to include an MRI and a CT scan, to establish a base line of her brain's agility. Absolutely, absolutely, Dr. Campbell couldn't agree more—the effusive phrasing that will also appeal to Izzy.

Antonia is holding her breath. Is it going to happen: Izzy will agree to get consistent, residential professional help? Antonia exchanges a glance with her sisters. On their faces those lifted eyebrows of incredulous cautious hope, part and parcel of their genetic package.

But wait! Izzy jabs a thumb in her sisters' direction. What about their "diagnosis"—Izzy air quotes—that I'm bipolar? There! She's acknowledged the elephant in the room. The sisters flash Dr. Campbell an SOS. But she ignores them. The woman probably understands she needs to befriend that elephant. Izzy relishes having elephants in the room. It's her preferred domestic pet, the sisters like teasing her.

Well, if the evaluation were to come up with that as a diagnosis, and I'm not saying it will, Dr. Campbell adds as Izzy's face has tensed with suspicion, even so, we would find a way to treat it.

I know what you're all up to! Izzy says in a beeping-metal-detector voice. She has uncovered their plot. You pump me full of meds, so that I'm "functional." I'd rather die than be a zombie!

But you have been on medications before. Dr. Campbell checks her notes.

On and off, Izzy says. And they were zero help.

That could be part of the problem, Dr. Campbell nods. You have to give them time. But hey, bottom line is this can only work if we work together. Our approach is based on participatory care. We want our patients to discover a new life worth living and learn to make better choices. She seems to be reading off some brochure. The sudden shift to the first-person plural. The professional-ese phrasing. Stay authentic, Antonia coaches the doctor internally. We are almost there.

It's the only way it can work, the doctor goes on. Many, many patients have been helped at Liberty House. Medications are key but Izzy is right. The meds have to be adjusted, carefully monitored. Often, it's a simple chemical imbalance in the system, as you well know, the doctor adds, a nod to Izzy, the professional colleague. As if the two women are conferring on their mutual patient, another Izzy, who sometimes goes rogue, loses self-control, needs their collaborative help.

Izzy has fallen silent, her dark-side-of-the-moon mood, which Antonia knows well from her own sojourns there. Slowly, Izzy raises her head in a canine tilt, sniffing the air, picking up a scent that won't allow her to proceed. She levels her gaze first at Dr. Campbell, then over at her sisters, sitting in a righteous trinity to her right. Antonia finds herself wishing that she had made a different seating choice. She had thought of it when they walked in the room, as she always does when visiting a therapist's office, convinced that the therapist has pegged each choice—couch or rocker or straight-backed chair or meditation cushion on the floor—with a corresponding disorder.

Mona and Tilly hold steady, returning their sister's piercing look with the long-suffering, loving expressions they perfected in childhood to respond to their

mother's rages. But Antonia has never been able to with-
stand Izzy's probing interrogations; her sister's eyes bore
through her many selves to that tender, unrehearsed self
that hasn't yet practiced and performed itself. Antonia
looks back, and she, in turn, pierces through her sister's
many self-presentations—the charming, cunning, impas-
sioned, flirtatious Izzys—past all the maneuvers that
have allowed her to outsmart her therapists and evade
treatment. But what Antonia sees unsettles her. She feels
a cold liquid entering her veins, as when she has been
put under at the hospital for some procedure or other.
She winces in anticipatory pain.

Izzy is beyond their reach.

I hear your words, she had said some weeks back
to Antonia on the phone. I hear them, but they don't
come through to me. What a horrible thought! Like that
Dickinson poem Antonia often taught, the plank in reason breaking, the speaker dropping down and down,
hitting a world at every plunge, never landing. *And
Finished knowing—then—*

The poem stopped mid-sentence. Below it only the
white blank of the page. This was Antonia's dragon,
why she had avoided too much contact with Izzy after
Sam's death: words, words, words, failing her.

I don't know, Izzy says, her head like a periscope

turning and looking around. I don't know. I think I'll give it a pass.

Tilly is the first to burst into tears. Please, please, Izzy, I'm begging you. I'll never ask for anything ever from you, I promise! Tilly has fallen on her knees, sobbing so hard that soon she is gasping for breath, bringing on her smoker's cough, a hacking, horrible sound, as if she is coughing up her very soul. The sight of her in such agony fells Mona, who drops to her knees, pulling Antonia down with her. What a sight before the cool-mannered psychiatrist with her diploma from Harvard on the wall. No wonder her patient exhibits extreme behaviors. The sisters are all nuts. But wait, maybe Dr. Campbell was present the day Dr. Vega lectured her medical school class on cultural sensitivity. This might be a Latina way of caring.

See what I have to put up with? Izzy jokes, flashing the doctor a collegial smirk.

But Dr. Campbell seems to have shifted allegiances. She will not settle for a glib response. I'd say your sisters really love you, she speaks with a wistfulness to her voice, as if this is a love she has yearned for and never known herself.

I guess then . . . Izzy takes a deep breath and lets out a surrendering sigh. I guess Love wins the day. The sisters lurch forward to hug her, cheerleaders whose down-on-their-luck team has finally won a game.

There is a flurry of phone calls: to the physician in charge of admission at Liberty House, the psychiatrist who will lead the team evaluating Izzy, the pharmacist for a prescription Izzy is to start immediately, a small dose, to settle her down. It is decided. Today being Friday, the weekend upon them, on Monday Izzy will report to this office and she and Dr. Campbell will walk across the green to the house that looks like an antebellum mansion to begin her soul spa.

Izzy stands, ramrod straight, clicks her heels together, and gives them all a salute. Antonia's heart sinks. Oh boy, oh boy, she thinks. This is not going to work.

Cuckoos in Kyoto

Emotions ran high, as they always did when the sisters gathered together. But despite its intensity, it had been a hopeful weekend, considering. Monday, at 10 a.m., by her own consent, Izzy would be admitted at Liberty House, a name she accompanied with air quotes.

Her sisters kept congratulating each other. They had pulled it off. "Monday, Monday," they sang out of earshot of Izzy. Of course, this treatment wouldn't be a magic bullet. Izzy had an illness that would need to be managed all her life. I told you guys, Mona said one too many times.

Izzy moped, packing and repacking her bags. What to take with her to the loony bin, she joked.

Remember, her sisters kept reminding her. You're not going to Siberia or a lockdown prison. You're free to go out if you need to.

Izzy responded with that look again, the one that had unsettled Antonia at the psychiatrist's office. She had something up her sleeve—Antonia was sure of it. Promise me, she confronted her sister straight on, that you're not going to . . . Should she name the unnamable? Put ideas in her sister's head? Instead she said, Promise me you won't break my heart. Izzy? Do you hear me?

I hear your words, but they don't come through to me, Izzy had said. Her voice, but without Izzy behind it.

Kaspar had taken off to Boston to see the Botticelli exhibit at the Isabella Stewart Gardner museum. Enjoy your madonnas! the sisterhood toodle-ooed, ushering him out, glad not to have him around to temper their temperaments. When Tilly, with Mona in tow to keep her company, stepped out for a smoking break, Antonia crawled in bed with Izzy, hoping to infuse her with a heavy-duty dose of sister comfort.

Do you really think I'm sick? Izzy asked, suddenly all there, her face inches away. It was impossible to escape those two searchlights beaming into Antonia's eyes.

Antonia didn't know what to say: she didn't want to dismiss Izzy's need for professional help. But she also didn't want her sister to feel damaged and diminished in any way. Who can speak to this? she addressed the pack of writers in her head whose work she had studied, taught, treasured, random lines spinning daily through her thoughts. Come on, guys! One of you, step up to the plate now. "Canst thou not minister to a mind diseased? Pluck from the heart a rooted sorrow?"

Ay, Izzy, Antonia crooned, rocking her sister in her arms. Here's what I think: life is hard. *Even in Kyoto, hearing—*

You're no help at all, Izzy said, shrugging off Antonia's embrace.

SEVERAL TIMES DURING the weekend, Antonia took a walk in the woods behind the hotel, down a small knoll to a brook, its shores lined with mossy boulders, the birds audible above the highway hum in the distance. Somewhere, perhaps at summer camp, where she had picked up most of her nature lore (what to do in a lightning storm, what to do about an allergic reaction to a bee sting), Antonia recalled having been told that, should she get lost in a forest, she was to locate a brook, or stream, or river, and follow it, as eventually it would lead to civilization. But what if she wanted to get away from civilization? Actually, the scenes in the hotel had to be the opposite of civilized: her sisters—not just Izzy—grandstanding, throwing tantrums, the emotional temperature at a continuous fevered pitch.

Antonia longed to escape, but this weekend especially, all hands had to be on deck. And anyhow, where could she go for peace of mind and heart? Was it the Buddha whose father had kept him closed up in the palace, so he wouldn't experience or be exposed to anything negative? Then the day came when his chariot driver took him for a ride outside the palace walls, and the young prince saw a sick man—or was it an old man? Whatever it was, the prince was profoundly shaken. Yes, even safe and sound in Kyoto, there was always that cuckoo cry.

During one of her walks that weekend, her cell phone had pinged with a text message. She had planned to ignore any such attempts to reach her—twenty minutes of total disconnect, for God's sake! But she had succumbed to the sly foot in the electronic door: I'm-just-going-to-quickly-check-and-see-who-it-is. Beth Trotter's message flashed on the screen. Estela in labor! No worries. She's doing fine. She asks about you all the time. Smiley face, heart, Dr. Trotter had signed off. Who would have guessed a couple of the emoticons Antonia so decried as lazy

shorthand—the intense need to find the right words—
would fell her own defenses? Antonia again felt that rush
of the maternal.

At dinner that night, Antonia informed the others of
the news. Izzy was eager for the details. Again, Antonia
was struck by how quickly her sister could forget her
own angst and enter into a stranger's situation. This
would stand her in good stead, this ability to put herself
in perspective.

What're you waiting for? Get going! Izzy com-
manded in her bossy voice. You can't leave her alone at
a time like this!

She's not alone, Antonia countered, and the hospital
has this translating device.

Izzy shook her head in a what-has-the-world-
come-to? way that recalled their mother in bafflement
over one or another of their Americanized behaviors.
Since when is it okay to outsource basic human presence? Please? Izzy asked sarcastically.

What about leaving you? Antonia answered. Who
is the most important one? Sometime during one of her
future visits, Antonia would tell Izzy the Tolstoy story with
the three questions. She might find it helpful, just knowing that even the world's geniuses struggled with choices
as they sought to live lives of purpose and meaning.

But you're not leaving me alone. Izzy gestured with her head at her sisters, who sat by with thumbtack looks on their faces—pinning Antonia back in her place among them. I already have two bodyguards. I don't need a third.

Thanks a lot, Mona pouted. In a flash, Antonia could see the ghost of Mona Past sweep across her baby sister's features. We have a life, too, you know? she added, turning on Antonia. You're not the only one with people who need you back home.

This is different, Izzy defended their sister. This girl doesn't speak English. And her boyfriend threw her out. And she's all of—what? Fifteen?

A slight exaggeration, which Antonia would normally have corrected, but she let it pass, hoping the error might mitigate her desertion if she decided to go.

Tilly and Mona glared at Antonia, their grievances momentarily bigger than their hearts. Their mouths twisted like their mother's in disapproval. Not that Antonia and Izzy didn't have their own self-interest in mind. Antonia was longing to get away, and Estela's situation gave her the excuse she needed, while still claiming the moral high ground of helping someone else. And Izzy? Only later would Antonia suspect her sister of wanting to get Antonia out of the way. The sister of church bells, the dutiful, vigilant sister on the pullout couch who'd wake up if anyone tried to slip by on her way to the bathroom with a handbag full of pills, while the others slept on. Later, they discovered Izzy had also raided their suitcases for whatever medications they'd brought along. Ingredients for her deadly cocktail.

Sunday, after a tense brunch, Antonia said her good-byes. She had finally appeased Tilly and Mona by pointing out that in a few days both sisters would be gone, back home, and she, Antonia, would be the closest-by sister on call.

Okay, do what you have to do, they finally said, a grudging blessing on her departure. And Antonia had driven off, feeling oh so relieved to be free of the sisterhood. But as she put more and more miles between herself and them, she wondered: What was it she was so eager to get back to? An empty house, which, unless she changed her mind about Estela, would remain empty? A bleak world of self-protections: did she really want to live in it? Everyone barricaded against the suffering of others, hoarding their investment in their privatized versions of reality, giving their indifference the spin they needed in order to live exonerated, their therapist-office noise machines drowning out the cuckoo's crying. What was the bird saying with its penetrating cries?

You must change your life, Rilke had written at the end of a poem her students always responded to.

So when do you change it? And how do you start? she pressed them.

ON THE DRIVE HOME, Antonia found herself playing back the moment in bed with Izzy. What should she have said to her sister? Was Izzy ill or not? As crazy as the world was, Izzy's flamboyant schemes sometimes seemed a soulful, if not sustainable, response. And in fact, Antonia felt some of the same inclinations, the wild energy, the dark moods, but she had found a place to put them: in her writing, in her students, in Sam. Each of those safeguards had fallen away. All she had left now were habits of self-discipline and control. What if she let go? Would she end up joining Izzy at Liberty House?

What's the worst that can happen? Antonia had asked Izzy during their bedded tête-à-tête, hoping to put the present situation into perspective. Now, for the first time since losing Sam, Antonia allowed herself to look that dragon in the eye. What if she threw herself into the deep end of her life? She felt a young woman's excitement at the thought of letting the universe take her where it will. But the temptation lasted only a minute before the reversal set in, and she found herself murmuring a lay form of St. Augustine's famous prayer, *Lord make me chaste, but not yet.*

Make me into the larger version of myself, Antonia prayed, but let's wait. Let's wait till tomorrow. Mañana, mañana, the punch line of all those ethnic jokes about lazy Latins that people used to openly tell that Antonia never thought were funny.

TOMORROW COMES. A mild Monday morning in early May is just beginning to dawn. Antonia is awakened from a deep sleep by the alarming sound of barking dogs.

She fumbles for her cell phone on the bedside table. A hysterical Mona is wailing at the other end. Oh my God! Oh Antonia, you're not going to believe this!

Antonia is now fully awake, sitting up in bed, looking out the window in one of those slow-motion moments right before the world is about to change forever into the pre- and post- of this particular moment: a soft, spring, watercolor light is being brushed across the sky, putting out the stars. The pines on the southern border of the property are swaying: the wind must be coming from the north. The trees on the far hills have leafed out, a bright emerald green, surrounded by the darker, more serene green of evergreens. The earth is still here, she keeps reminding herself as Mona sobs out the news that now there are only three left in the sisterhood.

Calm down now, calm down, Antonia keeps saying to the hysterical Mona on the other end of the phone. Surely, Mona is overreacting. What she is saying can't be true. Her sisters can so easily slip into hyperbole. Just like Mami. Mangoes falling near the mother tree.

Antonia's calm infuriates Mona. Oh my God! I can't believe you! She wants me to calm down, she hears Mona reporting to whoever is with her, probably Tilly. Mona has correctly repeated the content but not the terror that lies below the chilled surface of Antonia's words.

Come on, Mo-mo, you know what I mean. Okay, okay, I'm sorry, Antonia concedes. *Do not contradict the mad or the enraged*—the buried instruction again resurfaces. Just tell me, okay? What happened?

I told Kim to make Izzy hand over all her meds, not to give her a prescription and let her self-administer. Nobody ever listens to me! Mona weeps. She took everything she had, plus everything she could find. My painkillers, sleeping pills. Empty bottles all over the place.

When was this? Antonia asks. She has enough wit not to voice the obvious question: Where were you all while this was going on? But Mona must hear the church bells ringing in Antonia's tone of voice. She is instantly on the defensive. How were we supposed to hear her? She snuck into the bathroom while we were sleeping. By the time we woke up, she was totally passed out on the floor.

This will not do. Put Tilly on, Antonia says in a tight voice. She wants a better, second opinion on Mona's bad news.

But Tilly is even less coherent than Mona: animal howls and whimpers of unbearable pain.

Hello? A woman comes on the line. Antonia—her conditioning kicking in at crisis moments—assumes the woman is a nurse since she is female. This is Dr. Kane, the woman introduces herself. She sounds too young to be in charge of anybody's life. This must be her first gig out of medical school, the bottom-of-the-totem-pole, late-night-early-morning shift at the ER in a small hospital west of Boston.

Your sister is still alive, Dr. Kane answers Antonia's first question. For a moment, Antonia feels such immense relief she spews out, Thank you, oh, thank you! From now on, Antonia will choose only young doctors as a good luck charm. Sam's ER doctor, the kindly Dr. Wolcott, must have been pushing seventy-five.

The doctor is going through her checklist, as if she were being examined by a licensing board, all the things she has done to resuscitate her patient, IV, intubation, meds to stimulate heartbeat. All our efforts have failed, the doctor concludes, her voice almost a whisper. Your sister is being kept alive by mechanical means, which, if disconnected, would mean death within minutes.

Antonia's relief has been so fleeting, it feels cruel to have summoned it at all. But you said she was still alive, she reminds the doctor in the same peevish tone as she used when her mother went back on a promise.

Who is her next of kin? the doctor asks after a heavy pause. Does your sister have a living will?

In another, less horrible moment, Antonia would burst out laughing. Dr. Kane, of course, can't know that Izzy would be the last person to plan for such an eventuality. She couldn't even say where she'd be on any given day.

I've gathered she does not have a husband or any children? the doctor pursues.

She has us, the sisterhood.

I didn't catch that.

She has her sisters. And a ton of people who supposedly "love" her, Antonia adds. She already misses Izzy's air quotes.

So, you, her sisters, will have to decide what to do.

What do you mean *we* decide what to do? You're the doctor! Antonia is furious at the whole medical establishment. They let Izzy self-medicate. They let Sam die. Soon, they'll let her die, too. Shame on them!

I'm so sorry. Dr. Kane sounds genuinely sorry. In a few years the young doctor will have been coached on not using any such litigiously loaded phrasing that might imply error, apology.

Isn't there a chance she could recover? Antonia pleads with the woman. Come on, work with me on this one.

The damage to her brain is irreparable, the doctor says in a hushed voice, as if it is a secret they must all keep from Izzy.

But I'll give her whatever she needs! Antonia offers desperately. An organ, a blood transfusion. Where on earth did Antonia learn science? Also at summer camp? Izzy needs a new brain, a new heart, a second life. We have the same blood type, you know? We were always mistaken for twins growing up. Same frizzy-kinky hair they both detested and ironed, same knobby knees, same bony build.

Dr. Kane keeps saying, I'm so sorry.

This woman is no help at all! Will you just put her on?

Dr. Kane hesitates. Her patient is in no condition to talk.

Of course, Izzy can't talk! Antonia isn't a total science dummy. She knows what is possible. Just hold the phone to her ear, Antonia sobs, her anger washed out of her, weapons tossed on the ground.

Antonia listens to the rattle of the respirator, the beeping of monitors, her sisters weeping in the background. Ay, Izzy, how could you? is all she can think of saying. But she doesn't want her last words to her sister to be a scolding, raining on Izzy's cortege as in the past on her parades. Still, Antonia can't think of a single word to say. It's finally come: the frightening moment she has fought so hard to prevent, when not just the world but the words fall apart, and the plunge goes on and on and on.

IF YOU EVER need a transfusion or an organ, Antonia once offered Izzy in the dark of their shared bedroom, overcome with love for her older sister, remember you can always come to me.

Are you kidding? Izzy scoffed. Why would I want your cooties?

Antonia had been glad for the darkness, so Izzy couldn't see her tears. Here she was offering to risk her life for her sister and Izzy had turned her down. Why did Izzy detest her so? She wanted to ask, but she knew what her sister would say, Because you ask such stupid questions!

All their shared childhood, Antonia was convinced Izzy hated her, until that time in summer camp when Antonia was thrown from her horse during the big horse-show on parents' weekend. She lay in the dust, a trickle of blood coming from the back of her head, eyes closed, dead to the world. Izzy had jumped into the ring, wailing and pulling her hair and begging Antonia to come back to life. Please, please, oh, Toni, please don't die!

You were like a banshee, screaming your head off, their mother recounted. (Where on earth had their mother picked up the word *banshee*, mispronounced "bang-she"?) Antonia has no memory of the actual fall, but she recalls coming to and hearing Izzy's inconsolable weeping and delaying opening her eyes to savor this exquisite moment: Izzy loved her! A light came on in Antonia's life.

And now Izzy has put it out.

THE SEQUENCE IS a blur. There is the drive back to Boston that morning, a stay of four, five days, or is it more? They have changed hotels, too creepy to stay in the old one, the rug will have to be shampooed, the green vomit leaving the faintest stains, the management very kind when the sisters offer to reimburse them. There are arrangements to be made, papers to be signed, bills to be paid—*the expensive delicate ship . . . had somewhere to get to and sailed calmly on*; lines that used to be lifesaving—mantras to keep confusion at bay, string in this labyrinth—fly off, untethered, disconnected, yadda yadda yaddas of past meaning. There's a delay in getting Izzy cremated, as the coroner's office has gotten involved, for although it is not a crime to be missing even unto death by one's own hand, still, in one of those conundrums, law enforcement needs to know that the suicide was a suicide.

So it is that several weeks later, after Mona and Tilly have gone back to their respective homes, Antonia drives down again to pick up the ashes at the funeral home, returning the same day in the soft evening light, a tearjerker light if there ever was one, Izzy riding beside her in the passenger seat in a white box that weirdly reminds Antonia of Chinese takeout. Inside the satchel (PATTERSON & SONS: CELEBRATING LIFE, ONE FAMILY AT A TIME), there is a card with a white dove flying in a gauzy sky from the Donor Center acknowledging receipt of Izzy's organs. *You have given the gift of life. Thank you.*

You're welcome. Don't mention it. Yes, please don't mention it. Antonia jokes to Izzy's ashes beside her. All these niceties and euphemisms attached to the death of a person you love. Dr. Kane's astonishing verb, *harvest*, when she asked Antonia, who seemed the least distraught of the sisters, which wasn't saying much, What organs of your sister's should we harvest? Antonia pictured a combine like the ones Sam had pointed out in his native Nebraska cutting swaths in the amber waves of grain on what was left of his family's farm. Sam on his knees in his Vermont garden digging out his potatoes.

Take whatever you want! she had replied, her voice rising, a liberating cry. A strange hilarity had come over her. Antonia felt like a rebel throwing wide the gates of a barricaded city, the investments contained therein no longer privatized. She was sounding out of control, but why not splurge on the thrilling feeling of falling, falling, hitting a world at every turn—

Harvest away! Okay? OKAY? Antonia hollered even louder.

I'm so sorry. Dr. Kane said it again.

ELEVEN

As if

There have been times when Antonia's life seemed weirdly in sync with earthshaking events. She left her first husband on the very day of the nuclear meltdown at Three Mile Island. She and Sam married hours before the Tiananmen Square massacre, and the image of tanks plowing down young people, their outspread arms mirroring the embrace she was giving Sam, haunted her every year on their anniversary. The evening of the Haitian earthquake, while buildings tumbled, men, women, children crushed under rubble, her father died.

It was the opposite of that Auden poem about

suffering, how it takes place while someone else is opening a window or eating a piece of pie. A boy tumbles
from the sky just as an expensive delicate ship goes sail-
ing by. Her life, on the other hand, seemed to be riding
the coattails of the horror, the horror. And because each
public event was so devastating, her individual drama
seemed petty in comparison. It was a corrective: being
aligned to a world larger than her own. It put her puny
sorrows (and joys) in perspective.

Art reminds us that we're all connected, the guy eating the piece of pie, the ice skater going through the ice.
Her students all seemed intent on their note-taking, or
maybe, as in the poem, their minds were elsewhere: texting a boyfriend, complaining to their moms about their
English teacher going on and on.

But on the day Sam died, nothing of global signif-
icance happened. The world did not register his loss.
Even taking the long view, that date in history seemed
to have been a slow one. Everybody getting along, or at
least not killing each other over their differences.

So also, on the day when Izzy—rescued from herself, returned to the sisterhood, en route to the psychi-
atric residential care facility where she was to "discover
a new life worth living" and "learn to make better
choices" surrounded by a "supportive, complex, and

multilayered treatment team," as promised in the brochure copy—disappeared, this time for good, no omens
flew their red flags.

Maybe the time of meaningful synchronicities is
over? What happens after the worst that can happen has
happened? *After the final no there comes a yes—?*

Shut up! Antonia hollers at Stevens. Where was he
when she needed him to convince Izzy to hang on, wait
until today's *no* became tomorrow's yes?

DAILY, ANTONIA HEARS reports of the dying planet.
It's Nature's version of terrorism: terrible storms, rivers
bursting their banks, ice floes melting right under the
stricken polar bears. The world of impending doom is
no longer the province of the poor. Reefs gone, whole
species vanishing forever, those *dying generations—at
their song*, seabirds gorging on plastic, little villages
under the ocean, the waters rising. For Earth Day, one
of her former students invites Antonia on campus to a
rally advocating for divesting the college's endowment
of holdings in fossil fuel companies. One of the speakers,
a British journalist, speaks movingly of the task ahead.
Never mind the fossil fuel spent to get him across the
pond. What he has to say is not news to Antonia, but the
way he states the problem shakes her to the core.

We're being asked to do something mankind has never done before, he explains, the strain of emotion in his voice. We are demanding action for people who haven't been born yet. Moreover, because the areas that will be most affected by climate change are the poorest regions of earth, we are talking about the least-seen, least-represented group on our planet. We have to imagine these people into being, and then grant them rights, and then take unprecedented, society-wide action on that basis.

How can she not despair? Antonia wonders. As if responding to her thoughts, the speaker goes on to say that pessimism would be an ethical catastrophe. We have to live *as if*, in other words, by metaphor.

Antonia of all people should be able to do this. She has spent a lifetime working in those vineyards, taking leaps of metaphor, cultivating her own little plots of prose and poetry. She must live *as if* Sam, *as if* Izzy, *as if* her parents, tías, tíos, *as if, as if* . . . the list of losses goes on and on—as if it matters to them that Antonia not fall into one of her moods and join them.

A WRENCHING SPRING. Antonia feels like ordering all the shoots and bulbs, the crocuses, daffodils, tulips, to go back in the ground. Sam's rhubarb patch, asparagus bed, his clump of ramps he dug up in the forest. An effrontery to be confronted with so much new life.

Estela has contributed to these dying generations by giving birth to a healthy baby girl. But as if afflicted by the same despondency as Antonia, the young mother refuses to feed her infant or eat much of anything herself. She doesn't want anything to do with the newborn. She's not mine, Estela keeps repeating.

How can it not be hers? Dr. Trotter challenges. I saw that baby come out of her! Beth understands about the father. Still, it's not the baby's fault. ¡El bebé necesario la mamá! Dr. Trotter mangles the Spanish she remembers from high school.

But Estela is adamant. She doesn't want this strange baby. She wants another baby, Mario's.

They will have to be patient, the counselor at the Open Door Clinic counsels. After all, the new mother is a traumatized child herself. She will have to be taught how to care for her infant, care for herself. All it will take is a little patience, constant and consistent reassurances until she feels safe.

A little this, a little that, the diminutives of Spanish, one of the losses Izzy, now lost herself, often lamented about English.

Not a whole life, not a guardianship, just this present

crisis. All Antonia has to do is fish the boy fallen from the sky out of the water in that Auden poem about suffering. She can do that much, she decides.

You're on your own after that! Antonia practices what she will tell Estela once they are past this impasse.

Sorry, she keeps saying, not sure to whom. Izzy? Sam? But along with keeping alive her sister's nobility of soul and Sam's basic decency, the only short-lived immortalities they are likely to have, Antonia has to live the only mortal life she is sure to have.

If I try to be like you, who will be like me? Her therapist's grandmother's Yiddish sayings now live on in the mind of a stranger she could never have imagined as a child in the camps.

AND SO IN MID-MAY Estela moves in. The empty house fills with the messy busyness of two more lives, one with no sense of the divine division between day and night. With encouragement and the small incentives of extra cash for helping with this and that, Mario starts coming around. Antonia buys the Spanish-language package from the cable TV provider, 80+ canales en español, 120+ en inglés, not only to entertain Estela as she breastfeeds the baby on the couch but also to entice Mario to stay after his little jobs are done, his cash pocketed, to watch his programas and telenovelas on la doñita's big screen, a lot better than the small box with rabbit ears left behind in the trailer by former workers. From her study Antonia can hear the two teenagers cheering on their favorite teams or gasping at the antics of the narcotraficantes or falling silent when El Noticiero brings more distressing news from the border they once crossed.

Estela names the baby Marianela—a smart move, giving the little girl the name of the disgruntled boyfriend Estela hopes to woo back. Antonia's friends comment that Marianela is the spitting image of her namesake, whom they assume is the baby's father. But these are friends who aren't acquainted with many Mexicans, so it might well be a case of all people of a certain race or ethnicity looking alike to someone who doesn't share the same traits. In this case, though, they have a point. There's a strong resemblance—same pointy chin, same dimples and slight Asian slant to the eyes, not such a stretch in their small village that the biological father might well be a distant relation of Mario. Perhaps this resemblance or the fact that the baby endearingly takes to him, quieting when she is handed over—begins to soften Mario's tough stance.

Antonia seems more lighthearted herself, her friends comment, relieved. Everybody likes a resurrection.

Dinner party invitations increase. She's a better guest, Antonia guesses. Except when she gets started on the situation of undocumented workers in their very same county, carrying Vermont's dairy industry on their backs, or in Cassandra mode, on the looming death of the planet, Antonia can get as tiresome as poor dear Sam— her turn to ruin the lite mood at her friends' gatherings.

She has become friends with the much younger Beth Trotter by virtue of their common bond, looking out for Estela and her baby—a bond nonparent Antonia has never before experienced but often observed among moms in the playground, talking endlessly and unapologetically with each other about feeding strategies and toilet-training approaches and schooling options without feeling they're circumscribing everybody else's world in their sandbox.

Have you considered making this a more permanent arrangement? Beth asks one Saturday as they head to a workshop at the Zen Center.

Too many times! Antonia laughs, and leaves it at that. Given their destination today, Beth also lets it go.

Antonia has signed up for a series of six workshops Beth invited her to attend at the center, where she is a member. Couldn't hurt, Antonia encouraged herself. The workshops, Beth assured her, would not be hard-sell

Zen, not playing dress-up with an Eastern religion, but fun, relaxing activities: rock gardening, Tai Chi, ink drawing, and today's flower arranging. Bring your own vases and blooms, if you have them. Antonia harvests handfuls of flowers in the garden, hoping the teacher will enlighten her as to their names. But the teacher, an American woman with a placid face and closely cropped hair—perhaps a Buddhist monk or a cancer survivor?— rarely speaks. They are to circle their vases, breathing in, breathing out, observing the blooms, the grasses, their angles, this way and that, adjusting for balance. Antonia, accustomed to her own very different teaching style, where words and the structures made from them are the focus, nevertheless finds herself enjoying this quiet respite from the rigors of wordsmithing the world. *Let it be, let it be*, the lyrics play in her head. There she goes again, caught in the word thicket!

Unfortunately, this Saturday, Beth's question reboots the internal debate of what to do about Estela. *What is the right thing to do?* The question rings in her head, worse than church bells. The nodding peacock orchid, the stalk of prairie grass, the sticks from the woods beyond the outdoor Zen garden—she can't get her arrangement to balance.

Driving home, Beth asks how she enjoyed the class.

Too busy in here, Antonia cocks a finger at her fore-head. My mind killed it.

Sorry to hear that, Beth says, and soon she's hearing a lot more as Antonia voices her quandary: Estela, the baby, whether to or not to . . .

Finally, she says it: I'm just not up to it.

Well then, that answers it, Beth says with a certainty that settles the matter. No wonder Beth's flower arrange-ment garnered gratifying bows from their teacher today. It's all fine and dandy to be Mother Teresa, if you're Mother Teresa, her younger friend expounds.

If I try to be like you, then who will be like me? Is it also a Zen saying?

Might be. Beth shrugs. It's a magnet on my fridge. *Be yourself, everyone else is taken.*

Antonia laughs outright. Thank you, she says, and laughs again. This is therapy without the price tag—in other words, friendship.

Beth is absolutely right. No matter how worthy or commendable taking on Estela and her new family would be, when Antonia asks herself torturously, *What is the right thing to do?* The certainty is not there. What lies beyond the narrow path, the nibble, the sip, where the dragons be? Just because she doesn't yet know doesn't mean she should close down and settle for the joyless default. The earth doesn't need one more resentful, depressed sort. Having studied and taught stories and poems all her own life, it's now in her DNA, to want to give that life a shapely form, fill in the blank in the dangling line: *And Finished knowing—then—*

As if the fragile earth has not been informed of its imminent demise, the summer unfolds. It seems every living thing that can bud and bloom bursts open, spraying the air with fragrances, holding on tight to the earth with roots that sometimes poke through the ground wanting to see the immense blue sky, too. The evenings are long, the light lingering like a child fighting sleep to have one more bit of the day gone by. Antonia sits for hours in the garden, half believing she can hear the kernels of corn plumping in their husks, the vines inching up on their trellises, the bees raiding the blossoms. She is waiting like a numb animal for the warmth to penetrate, as in childhood after a bad fall when she would lie very still on the pavement, before the pain hit and the fear, waiting to learn what she had done to herself, what might be broken, whether she was already dead or not.

Daily, she checks in on her two sisters. How's it going, baby sisters? They argue over an appropriate ceremony for Izzy. Do they hire a hot air balloon and throw handfuls of her ashes over the side? Do they go out on a canoe—Izzy loved canoes—to the middle of a lake, scoop up handfuls of ashes, and throw them over the side? Enjoy! Anything they come up with falls short of the extravaganza that Izzy would have devised. But wasn't that over-the-top behavior part of her illness?

Do you believe me now? Mona has asked Antonia, not with the triumphant note of the vindicated, but with the defeated voice of someone who wishes she hadn't been right. A pyrrhic victory, Antonia had explained to her students, is one that exacts such a heavy toll that winning looks an awful lot like losing. A definition of life on our dying planet, Antonia can now report back to them.

Since the sisters can't agree on a ceremony, Antonia divvies up Izzy's remains, as the official handlers of the dead call them, each sister getting her doggie bag to do with as she sees fit. Antonia has no idea what she will do with hers. She thinks about scattering the ashes in the garden, but that's what she did with Sam's ashes. Izzy would want something more original, all her own.

Late summer, the sisters gather to go through Izzy's things in the storage shed she had rented when she sold her house. They embarrass themselves with their grabbiness. They all want the Russian doll nesting juice glasses, the lamp with the fabulous shade that lights up into a swarm of butterflies, Izzy's funky hats and faux fur wraps, her beaded handbag, her large art nouveaux Buddha lounging on his side. They can't have Izzy, so they want as many of her things as they can wrangle from the others, only to find that once they haul the loot home, they can't bear to have it around, reminding them that Izzy is gone. Antonia holds a yard sale, all of Izzy's treasures, many of Sam's, throwing in freebies whenever anyone bought something. To this day, Antonia will spot a townsperson wearing a Cornhuskers baseball cap or a flashy yellow shawl and catch herself lifting a hand, on the point of calling out, SAM! IZZY!

They are here, albeit a little scattered, a matter of dispersal. Antonia never knows where they will turn up next. You really believe that? Mona asks, her sensible mind at war with her desperate yearning to fill the hole in her heart.

Bless the spirit that makes these leaps, Antonia quotes Rilke, sounding just like that widow therapist in the podcast, *for truly we live in what we imagine*.

I guess you're right, Mona says tentatively.

TWELVE

Harvest

Once again, Antonia is driving to Boston. A trip she has made often in the past few months. At the edge of town, she passes several houses with flags flying; a yellow ribbon encircles a tree with matching leaves. September 11, she is well aware. No synchronicities, please, she prays. Let the troubles end now.

This morning on NPR, along with commemorative recollections by survivors and family members of those who died, there are reports of hurricanes battering the Caribbean and Chiapas, luckily an area southwest of where Estela and Mario hale from—although how can she utter the adverb *luckily* with dozens injured and thousands homeless? At the border, mothers and fathers seeking asylum are being turned away, or if they are lucky enough to cross, unluckily their children are then taken away.

Along with those towers, the world as Antonia knew it has collapsed. *Wandering between two worlds, one dead, / the other powerless to be born*—so many of the words and works she has spent a lifetime teaching seem now prescient and apropos of what is coming to pass. At least, Antonia tries to console herself, neither Izzy nor Sam are having to live through these broken times.

But they are also missing the swallows, a large twittering flock darkening the evening sky as they flew off the roof of Roger's barn yesterday; missing the early morning view outside her bedroom window, the mist dispelling, the far hills emerging, taking shape, having survived the night; missing the intricate spiderwebs on the barbed-wire fence, their dewed filaments jeweled with light; missing the brisk charge in the air as the wind sharpens, the maples turning red and gold, the kids walking to school with their brand-new paraphernalia, little battalions of bright colors, their shouts and laughter recalling a childhood world gone by. The garden is still flourishing with whatever late flowers self-seeded from the previous summer: asters, cosmos, sunflowers, and nameless blooming things about which she can no longer ask Sam, What's this called? Earlier this summer, with help from Mario and José, Antonia did plant a few crops—potatoes, sweet corn, her favorite pole beans—Estela pitching in from time to time, her baby in a sling reminiscent of those the women in her village have improvised for centuries out of fabric, this one bought online at four, five times the cost, none of the profit going back to where the template came from.

A few days ago, Antonia delved into the soil and dug out Sam's potatoes—she still calls them Sam's, even though this year her own hands planted and harvested them. Will she ever use that verb again without thinking of Izzy's body, split open, her heart, kidneys, liver placed in a cooler to be flown across the country to wherever someone awaited her sister's gift of life?

Enjoy! Izzy would always say whenever she unveiled one of her lavish gifts, her extravagant surprises: eighty-three orchids, a kidney, a liver, a heart. Enjoy, enjoy!

Today, Mario is riding beside her, all cleaned up in an ironed shirt and jeans. He has been talking nonstop, excited, full of plans, seemingly unaware of the other passenger in the back seat, whom periodically—when Antonia can get a word in edgewise—she tries to loop in.

¿Cómo están? Antonia glances in the rearview at Estela and her baby, playing a clapping game, Estela bringing the tiny hands together while chanting: *A la una yo nací, a las dos me bautizaron, a las tres supe de amores y a las cuatro me casaron. At one I was born; at two, baptized; at three I fell in love; at four I married; at five I had a child; at six my child died* . . . and so on, all the way to midnight when the speaker succumbs to cancer, and her life is done. It's a terrible song, circumscribing the little girl's life even before she has gotten started.

¡Por favor! Antonia protests. Let's sing Mari some other song. Even in Spanish with someone else's kid, Antonia wants the words to be right. *We live in what we imagine.*

They settle on "Cielito Lindo," Estela rocking her baby to the rhythm, laughing each time Marianela makes a gurgling sound. She already knows how to sing! the mother exclaims, showering her little genius with kisses. It's comforting to witness this backseat tableau of teenage Madonna and child. Estela's maternal feelings have more than kicked in.

Antonia is driving the family first to the Mexican consulate to pick up Estela's expedited passport, then to Logan for the flight to Mexico City, where they will transfer to Mexicana and a flight to Tuxtla Gutiérrez,

Chiapas, then take a three-hour bus ride, the baby bawling, the weary youngsters hungry and irritable themselves. With la doñita's help, Mario will be opening an equipment repair shop in Las Margaritas, and Estela will go back to school to be a "norsa"—a quick language learner, her Spanish is now speckled with Spanglish. Once settled, they will be marrying, the gift already given to pay for la fiesta—plans Antonia is not sure will be kept, but she has handed over the controls of others' lives into their own hands. She has promised to attend the wedding, bringing along some ashes to scatter as a "blessing." Given her interest in the girl's situation, Izzy would approve.

They have just left town, heading south on Route 7 when—her sheriff-fund donor sticker notwithstanding—Antonia sees the flashing lights of a state trooper's cruiser in her rearview mirror. She pulls over, her heart thundering in her chest. Tranquila, tranquila, she reminds herself. If dogs can smell out fear, as Mona has often told her, so can law enforcement. Objects in the mirror are supposed to be closer than they appear, but this trooper is taking forever to walk the short distance from his cruiser to the window Antonia has lowered.

She smiles agreeably at the young officer, as if he's just paying them a visit on this sunny September morning. Hi, there! she greets him.

The officer nods in response. Did she know she was going forty-one in a thirty-mile zone?

Forty-one! He's exaggerating. Surely not more than forty. But along with not contradicting the mad and furious, it's also a good idea not to argue with law enforcement. Lessons from childhood in a dictatorship. I didn't mean to, officer. I'm so sorry.

The officer asks for Antonia's license and registration, then heads back to his cruiser to check them out. In days gone by, Antonia would have pulled out her cell phone at this point and called Sam. You know the speed limit there is thirty, he would have chided her.

Just as well then not to have the option of calling him, though the scolding would have come with a rescue, a package deal. Someone has to be the grown-up in the room, Sam always used to say whenever Antonia would panic about a fix they were in. It's up to Antonia now to reassure her two passengers, Mario next to her, and Estela in back with the baby. They have gone very still and silent, as if they could somehow make themselves vanish. No se preocupen, she keeps repeating. Todo va salir bien. They were headed for Mexico anyway. The glass half full. The silver lining. Attitudes and approaches pulled out of the old chestnut trunk like dress-up clothes to distract the scared children in her care.

In the rearview mirror she watches as Estela squeezes her eyes shut—that grimace right before a face crumbles in tears. Ay, doñita, por favor, Estela wails, clutching her baby. While Antonia was listening to NPR all summer, Estela was taking in all those reports on Noticieros Televisa about la crueldad en la frontera. Children being separated from their mothers and fathers.

¡No va a pasar! Antonia states categorically with such Beth-like assurance that Estela instantly stops crying.

The officer is back, Antonia's documents in hand. Good news: everything has checked out; he's going to give her a break—a cat and mouse move—because at the same time he's releasing her, he is bending down to peer inside. His face is so close, Antonia can smell milk on his breath, his former farm-boy breakfast habits still intact. His skin is so pale, she can see the tiny capillaries just below the surface. A phrase, too pedestrian to be anyone's famous words, runs through her head: *his mother's son.* Unaccountably, Antonia's heart floods with tenderness at this untimely moment, just as in her long-ago hormonal youth, she'd feel herself inconveniently getting turned on at an inappropriate time, during a final exam, a job interview, on the checkout line at a store.

So, can we go now? Antonia asks far too tentatively.

The young officer hesitates, his eyes scanning the inside of the car, a brown male passenger in front, a brown girl cowering in the backseat, hugging a tiny doll—or is it a baby?—dressed in a frilly outfit. His face tightens with authority. One hand on his holster, perhaps anticipating trouble. What about your passengers? he asks Antonia.

What about them? Antonia smiles prettily. The girl who could get out of a scrape using her wiles has long disappeared from her old woman's face. Oh, them? I'm taking them to the consulate in Boston and then the airport. They're going back to Mexico. She cannot offer to show the officer their airline tickets as proof because she purchased them online. But they'll soon be over the mountain and through the woods and into the air, headed for home, beyond his jurisdiction.

Do you have any identification? the officer asks Mario, who looks to Antonia to translate.

He has his passport, Antonia explains. Will that do, officer? Of course, she knows it will only do if there is a USA visa stamped inside, which she is sure there isn't. But perhaps the officer won't notice; perhaps he missed the training session when ICE came and informed local law enforcement on the finer points of the customs and immigration laws.

Let me see what he has. The officer pauses. They're related? Husband and wife?

Soon to be, Antonia offers. The more she can make them sound like a family, the better she believes it will go for them all.

And the baby, theirs? the officer adds, pointing to Mario.

Soon to be, Antonia replies, before realizing how that must sound. I mean, soon as they get married, it will be official. She hands over Mario's passport, hoping the officer won't ask what he asks for next.

Hers, too.

Estela has no passport yet. She has a consular ID and the receipt from when the Mexican consulate came up from Boston with its mobile unit last month, and Estela applied for her passport. Rather than take a chance of it not arriving on time for her travel, they opted for going to pick it up at the consulate before the flight later today. Antonia explains all this to the officer, availing herself of only one teensy lie. Estela *lost* her passport and the replacement is waiting for them in Boston.

She can tell the officer is not happy about this—the capillaries on his cheeks flood with blood, two pink patches, a blushing look that in a different context Antonia would find endearing. He collects the proffered documents and heads back to his cruiser. Estela is again sobbing, this time so hard she is gasping for breath, and sensing her mother's fear, Marianela has begun to wail as well.

You have to stay calm for your baby's sake, Antonia admonishes.

Ay, pero, doñita, ¿Y si se la llevan?

No one is taking Mari, Antonia asserts. She decides not to add "over my dead body." It's not a Spanish idiom anyhow.

Would ICE really separate Estela from her baby? How can they? Estela is herself a minor. More likely, Mario will be deported, and perhaps precede mother and child to Mexico. What ICE will do to her, Antonia is not sure. Transporting aliens—there was an article in the local newspaper about a farmer and his wife being stopped with Lourdes Morales in the car. Lulu! Antonia doesn't know what happened to the couple, but Lulu ended up briefly in the local jail, under the purview of Sheriff Boyer, before ICE came to collect her and transport her to a detention center in Boston. In the interim, Sheriff Boyer asked Antonia if she would come in and translate for him.

Tell her not to worry; no one's gonna hurt her.

Ask her if she's got her paperwork in order.

Ask her if I can pick up some special food she'd like?

The sheriff had commented to Antonia that Lulu hadn't touched any of the jail meals. Not that he was surprised. Someone whose tasty food had been all the rage.

Tell her I'm real sorry about all this.

They were talking in his office, after Antonia's interview with Lulu in the visiting room. His intercom crackled constantly with static voices, deputy officers reporting in. At one point, the sheriff had to take a call, shielding the mouthpiece to whisper, The Feds. Antonia used the time to look around the room: guns, stacks of forms, photos of Sheriff Boyer with all the muckety-mucks in town. Her eyes suddenly caught on a small bottle of red nail polish on his blotter. The intriguing detail that opens a door to another's soul. Was Sheriff Boyer into cross-dressing? She checked his nails for residue chips or traces of his secret. None. But then, he was a cop. He had to know how to get rid of evidence.

Before she left the jail, she couldn't resist asking, What's the nail polish for? She lifted her chin to point to the bottle. Someone—was it Izzy?—had said that was a Dominican way of pointing.

Oh that, Sheriff Boyer chuckled. That's how I paint my dummy bullets for target practice. Wouldn't want one of my officers to pick up the wrong kind for their ammunition.

The same protective attention to detail had driven him to call Antonia, to ask Lulu what she might want.

What she wants is the laws changed, Sheriff. She wants to keep cooking her enchiladas and selling them so she can build a house that will not tumble when the next hurricane hits Mexico.

THEY WAIT FOR the state trooper to come back. The minutes tick by. Some glitch has come up, Antonia is sure of it. Sure, enough, she sees lights flashing, as another squad car races past the first cruiser and pulls onto the shoulder ahead of her own car. Oh boy, they are in deep trouble if the first officer has decided to call in reinforcements. Now she, too, feels like joining the wailers in the back seat.

¡Oigan, mi gente! Antonia calls their tense trinity to order. We have to stay calm, okay? She levels a look at Mario, who has reached for the door handle. No running away! Or the next thing they know the police will be firing warning shots in the air, and then, it's anyone's guess. It happens all the time in cities and every once in a while in sleepy rural towns. Unarmed men with dark skin holding cell phones or car keys that look suspiciously like weapons have been shot to death.

Nothing we can do but pray. As if she has spoken

literally, Estela and Mario bow their heads, intoning the prayer they learned by heart at their mothers' knees, entranced by the cadence even before they could understand the meaning of the words, no less the mystery they hoped to summon forth. *Santa María, madre de Dios . . .*

Looking out her windshield, Antonia has to laugh at her own cynicism. Feet first, followed by his hefty torso, Sheriff Boyer emerges from the second cruiser. He knocks off his hat on the rim of the door, stoops to pick it up, slowly straightens, red-faced, and heads toward them. The expression on his face is unsurprised; he already knows Sam's widow has been caught speeding out of town with two aliens in her car.

He stops at her window, glances inside, craning his neck to include them all. Hola, he greets the occupants, who reply in a hushed chorus, Hola. Doing a little speeding? he levels his gaze at Antonia, a pretend reprimand.

Sorry, I guess I wasn't keeping track, Antonia apologizes again. She explains the rush. I need to get these two folks to the consulate and then the airport in Boston, or they'll miss their flight back to Mexico.

There, she's made it perfectly clear: she can get this troubling pair out of his hands, pronto, as well as add to the coffers of the DMV. Just give her her ticket and Antonia'll be on her way. Win-win situation. No?

Let me see what I can do. Sheriff Boyer nods at each one in turn, although only one of his listeners understands his words. But like all who live in the shadows, Mario and Estela are fully fluent in tones of voice, facial expressions. They sigh with relief at the sheriff.

Cute little bambina, the sheriff adds. Got some good lungs on her. He nods at the hysterical baby, who has been handed over to the front seat to see if Mario can work his magic.

Antonia watches the sheriff stride toward the first cruiser, wagging his head, as if he's tired of all of them, including his young colleague for his overzealous ticketing of a minor speeding incident. Antonia overhears the back and forth, a good cop / bad cop routine she knows all too well. This time she is rooting for the good cop to win out.

¡Mira, mira! Mario is pointing out something to the baby he's been bouncing on his knee. ¡Un avioncito! At first, Antonia thinks Mario is just trying to distract the crying baby. But she sees it, too. Up in the sky the glint of a jet is leaving a gratifyingly foamy contrail.

Marianela blinks, peering into the sky. For a blessed moment, the car goes silent. Antonia watches as the speck in the air crosses her windshield and disappears into a bank of clouds. Just then, the first cruiser pulls back onto the road and races away as if in hot pursuit of other fugitives aboard the tiny plane.

Sheriff Boyer slaps the back side of her car as he approaches her window.

You're good to go, he says to Antonia, handing her back the documents the trooper had requested. Then addressing her passengers, he adds, Hasta la visa. Antonia has to bite her lip to keep herself from correcting his mistake.

Hey, hold on a sec! He stops her before she has shifted into gear and pulled away from the shoulder. He nods toward the back window and its outdated sticker. I see you haven't given yet this year. It takes Antonia a moment to know what on earth the man is talking about.

Japanese repair technique

Consider *kintsugi*, the mild-mannered, soft-voiced Asian man begins the last workshop in the Zen series. His skin is brown and smooth as a nut released whole from its shell. Antonia wishes she could take him home, a lucky charm to keep her safe from all the dragons.

A Japanese repair technique, he explains. They have gone around the circle, each person giving her or his name. They are mostly females, Antonia notes, their teacher appending *teacher* to each one's name. Antonia Teacher is next to last before their teacher, who introduces himself as No Teacher. The class nods reverently.

A joke, No Teacher says, giggling like a child being tickled.

He holds aloft a serving platter as if he is waiting for them to bid on it. Then, shockingly he knocks the plate against a nearby rock in the pebble garden they learned to rake into patterns last Saturday. The group gasps, but the small man throws back his head and laughs, then kneels to collect the broken pieces. A few of the attendees come forward to help, but No Teacher bows to each one.

Is unnecessary, he says in the same playful voice.

In reassembling the platter, No Teacher will not be using transparent glue and attempting to hide the broken places. He gestures toward a lineup of five bowls on a low table, then tilts each one in turn to display its contents: one filled with a thick amber lacquer, another with gold powder, a third with a clear liquid that smells like turpentine, one with plain water. The largest vessel is empty, and in it he mixes the lacquer and gold powder, adding several drips of water. He pulls up a footstool and sets to work, reuniting piece with piece, dabbing his brush into the gleaming paste, until the platter is mended, the gold intersecting grid showing where it has been broken. No Teacher clamps the platter firmly between his hands, waiting for the glue to set. Is time to meditate, he says, closing his eyes.

Antonia closes her own eyes. She sees herself falling out of the sky like that boy in the poem she taught maybe a hundred times in her teaching life. All the things she is breaking in her plunge are being reassembled, a painter's brush correcting her errors, the lines of repair showing up as lines in poems and stories she has loved, evidence of the damage done.

She should not be having these thoughts. She should be meditating.

Is whole, No Teacher remarks, waking her from her reverie, beaming his transfixing smile, his face a scratch-pad of wrinkles. He holds up the repaired platter. For a moment, Antonia fears he will smash it into pieces again.

The platter goes around their circle, each one tracing the ridged gold lines, the damage made visible, the platter repaired. It tells a story. That it has been broken.

Is beautiful, No Teacher concludes.

These fragments I have shored against my ruins . . .

. . . Shantih   shantih   shantih

—T. S. ELIOT, *The Waste Land*